A Measure of Breath

A Measure of Breath

MARK RICHARD ROBINSON

RESOURCE *Publications* • Eugene, Oregon

A MEASURE OF BREATH

Resource Publications
An Imprint of Wipf and Stock Publishers
199 W. 8th Ave., Suite 3
Eugene, OR 97401

www.wipfandstock.com

PAPERBACK ISBN: 979-8-3852-5608-2
HARDCOVER ISBN: 979-8-3852-5609-9
EBOOK ISBN: 979-8-3852-5610-5

VERSION NUMBER 10/16/25

For Tessa
who walked with me through the deep, always to the light.

"I will serve the LORD my God, and God will bless my bread and my water and remove sickness from the midst of me."

— EXODUS 23:25, AUTHOR'S TRANSLATION

Contents

Beneath the Skin

I know now that victory is not the absence of wounds. Victory is the body, battered and remade, marked by the wars it has fought. Victory is breath that does not come easy, a lung that has forgotten how to stretch, the cruel joke of survival—a heart that beats but remembers too many battle rhythms. But what they do not tell you—what no one ever tells you— is that some battles do not end when the war is declared over.

The doctor told me the cancer was gone, retreated into remission. I had beaten it. I praised God for this victory. I had won. Twenty years have passed since that declaration. Twenty years of marking each year, each test result, each breath as another milestone, another stone placed on the altar of my survival. And only now did the doctor name what my body has known all along. That there are scars of victory. Remnants that linger to remind you even as you try to forget.

The doctor's words made the lingering scars seem like a gift. As if a wound that does not kill you is a blessing. As if breathlessness is simply a reminder of strength. As if all suffering must be rewritten as something noble.
But how do I see it?

Survival is a thing that lingers; we do not walk out of the fire and leave the ashes behind. The body keeps an account, a detailed ledger, that reminds you pain has a memory—that nothing truly vanishes, no matter how you try to forget. And I wonder now, not just what has been lost, but what more my body might yet take from me. Will it fail me in a moment of need? Will I stand before a congregation only to fall silent, breathless, undone?

So when I wake, lungs tight like a clenched fist, I wonder: Is this what the victors feel? Is this how the body remembers? I think of those who came before me, those who broadened their shoulders for me to stand on. What of the battles they fought? What wounds did they carry forward, sewn into their bones, passed from mother to child? Passed on to future generations. What of their scars and the scars that I do not wear but still bear? This is survival. But survival doesn't always mean you are winning. By God's grace, winning comes in various forms. So tell me, what does it mean to win when I still struggle to breathe?

The air is sharp with morning cold as I step onto the platform. The station is a place of motion, of urgency, but my body no longer moves with urgency. The burden of my backpack digs into my shoulders, the duffel bag swings heavily at my side, and I can already feel the warning signs. The tightening in my chest. The way my breath comes short.

The steps to platform 1 loom before me. And I take a deep breath. They are just a few, but enough to remind me that my body is no longer a thing that obeys. I place my foot on the first step. Exhale.
The second.
Inhale.
The third.
Already, I feel the pull of something deeper than exhaustion. I grip the railing because I need to be steady and because I do not want them to see. Those around me, the morning travelers, the ones with strong lungs and unbroken bodies. I do not want them to see the way my knees falter—my uncontrollable gasping. I do not want them to pity me. Worse—I do not want them to fear that I might fall.
One more step.
One more.

I reach the top, swallowing the air greedily, forcing stillness into my face, masking the tremor in my hands. The train is coming. And I make my way down now to platform 1. I can't walk any faster, I can't run to ensure I don't miss the train, but I can move with purpose. I will not miss the train; I will be late if I do. So I cannot, I must not. There is more at stake than punctuality. There are expectations, my name on a program, my voice expected in rooms that echo with worship and argument. I watch the train approach, steel and glass, and I think about the journey ahead. A three-day meeting, hours away— a gathering of ministers, of voices raised in praise and theology. They are expecting me. I am required to attend. So yes, I will go. I will board the train. I've made it just in time. When I arrive, I will sit among my colleagues and contribute, even if my body demands that I remember survival is not the same as healing.

The train doors slide open.

I step inside.

And for one terrifying moment, the world tilts. The floor is too far away, my breath is too thin, and the press of my scars bears down on me like a closing hand. I think— this is it. This is the moment I fall. Should I remain on this train? Do I need to get off?

I grip the nearest rail, steadying myself, forcing my lungs to remember their purpose. My seat is just ahead. But I wait, not wanting to sit close to any other traveler for fear of feeling closed in, claustrophobic, panicked because I'm struggling to catch my breath. I stay close to the doors. The train moves. Then slowly, I move forward, each step measured, each breath controlled.

I sit.

And so does my mind, spinning, traveling, remembering.

I think of the long nights spent in the quiet, the way suffering turns time into a slow, relentless thing. There was a moment— many moments—when I did not know if I would wake the next day. A moment when the walls of the hospital room seemed too small, the heaviness of my own body too much, the sound of my own heartbeat a reminder that even survival can feel like a battle. I think of the prayers I whispered in the night, the ones that did not feel like prayers at all. They felt like demands, like bargaining, like anger wrapped in desperation. I think of the verses I recited because they were the only words I had left. "Your word is a lamp to my feet and a light to my path."(Ps 119:105) The path is not always clear. The lamp does not always reveal the whole road—only the next step. And sometimes, even that light feels too dim to trust. This verse does not promise ease. It does not promise a road free of obstacles, a journey untouched by suffering. It does not promise that the body will not break, that the scars will not form, that the breath will not become labored. What it does promise is presence—divine presence. A flicker of light in the thick of the night, a guide when the body and spirit feel like they cannot move forward. I think about those who have journeyed before me, the ones whose bodies bore the burden of history, whose victories were laced with wounds, whose very breath was an act of defiance. Their survival did not mean they were free from suffering, but they moved forward, nonetheless. By faith. By grace. By the light that may not have illuminated every shadow but was still enough to keep them going.

So, what does it mean when the victory does not feel like triumph? When survival is not the absence of wounds but the bearing of them? The Word reminds me that I am still on the path. That even when my breath is short and my body falters, I am still moving. That the strain I carry— the memory, the pain, the endurance—is not proof of my weakness but of my witness.

The light does not erase the shadows. It does not erase the scars. But it does mean that even in the lingering ache of survival, I am not walking alone. And perhaps that is the victory— not in the unbroken body, but in the presence of a God who walks beside me, even when my steps are slow, even when my breath is shallow, even when I do not know what waits beyond the next bend in the road.

Not once did I lose faith. I never did. Not once. Not when my body withered under treatment. Not when my lungs first began to betray me. Not when I lay awake at night, breathless, pleading, not for my life, not for my survival, but for help to bear this affliction. Help that my family would cope.

Faith was never the question.

Faith is not certainty.

Faith is stepping forward even when the way is unclear.

Faith is breathing, even when it hurts.

The train moves forward, carrying me toward the meeting, toward the expectation, toward the work that still needs to be done. I wonder if they will notice. The others— the ones waiting for me, will they see the way my body has changed, and the way my breath comes in measured sips rather than full, effortless gulps? Will they understand the toll of survival, the cost it exacts, the way it marks you in ways that never truly fade? Or will they only see the victory? Will they look at me and call me blessed, because they do not know that some blessings feel like burdens? That some victories feel like losses. That survival is not the absence of wounds.

The train moves, the world outside a blur of motion, and I let myself breathe, not deeply, not fully, but enough. For now, it is enough.

The Weight We Carry

10:00 AM

The weight of my bags is nothing compared to the weight of memory. The train hums beneath me, a steady rhythm, a metronome to the thoughts unraveling in my mind. I shift the backpack at my feet, feeling its presence like something alive, something with history stitched into its seams. I have carried this bag for years. It has seen hospital rooms and church altars, worn pews and border crossings. It has been my companion in times of strength and weakness alike. And yet, no matter how many miles it travels with me, it cannot lighten the burdens I carry within. I press my hand against the material, feeling the familiar weight. And then—as though summoned by the pressure of my fingers—I remember the letter. I retrieve it from my backpack, the paper worn at the edges, creased from being folded and unfolded too many times. A letter I have not read in full, nor have I had the courage to face. I hesitate, then glance at the opening line. It reads,

"I don't know why I'm writing. Maybe because there's no one left to listen. Maybe because silence has never suited me, and yet now it is all I have." Those words sit heavily in my lap, heavier than the paper that carries them. An unexpected letter, an unexplained letter. A voice from the past, one I had not thought to hear again—not like this. What had happened to silence him? What truth had bent his voice to confession? I read the first line again. Then again.

The heaviness of it presses against me, not in what it says, but in what it does not. There is something unfinished here, something waiting in the silence between the words. I fold the letter before I can read further, pressing the creases down with slow, deliberate hands. I will not read all of it. Not yet. Not here. Not while the train hums beneath me—not while strangers move around me, they who are unaware of the shift in my world.

What if reading further unravels something I've only barely held together? And so I think of the letter writer, Austin, of what little I know and of what I do not know at all. A colleague. A man whose voice I have heard in prayer, whose presence I have felt in rooms where scripture was opened and debated. A man who once stood with me in places where faith was supposed to be enough. But faith does not prevent harm. It does not make us immune to the burden of our own failings. He says he has no one left to listen. That silence has become his only companion. I wonder what he means by that. I wonder what in truth he has done. And I wonder why, of all people, he has written to me.

The train hums beneath me, a low vibration threading through the seat, through my bones. Outside, the world slips past in a blur, the countryside rolling into itself, fields stretching toward a sky heavy with the promise of rain. I should have read Austin's letter at home, in the quiet of my study, where its presence might have settled in more gently. But I read it here instead, amidst strangers and movement, and now it will not leave me. I fold the letter carefully and slip it back into my bag, but the words remain, echoing in my mind.

"I have sat in those rooms before, where judgment is passed, spoken words I thought were wise, nodded in agreement and called it justice."

I was in some of those rooms too. Not as often as Austin, not with the same authority, but I was there. And yet, in all my time sitting beside him, listening to him speak with conviction about right and wrong, did I ever suspect? Did I ever see a hint of the ruin that would come? And if I did see—what kind of man does that make me?

Memory is an unreliable thing. It reshapes itself, presses events into new shapes to fit the knowledge we now hold. If I tell myself I never saw anything, am I absolved? Or am I merely choosing not to look back too closely? Austin was not just a man of faith; he was a man of certainty. A man who stood before the congregation and spoke about sin, about righteousness, about the burden of choice. And now, the choices he made have brought him here, to this letter, to this reckoning. There was a time when Austin's presence in the church was one of authority. His words held significance, his voice steady, firm in conviction. He was a man others turned to for guidance, and for years, I trusted his discernment. Yet, there were moments—fleeting , insignificant at the time—a glance across the room, a hesitation in his speech, the way his attention would settle—almost imperceptibly—on her.

And now, I wonder if every hesitation I ignored was a warning I failed to heed. I remember the woman. A leader from his church. I have met her, spoken with her, but never thought much beyond that. She was devoted to the congregation, serious about her work, respected. Now, in the wake of what has come to light, I try to recall if there had been anything then, something small, something I might have dismissed.

Once, at a gathering after a service, I remember Austin speaking with her. It was nothing unusual, two leaders in conversation, but there was a moment, brief but striking, when their laughter came too easily, when the space between them seemed to shrink. I had thought nothing of it at the time. But was that because there was truly nothing to see, or because I had not been looking?

Outside, the world continues its motion, landscapes slipping past in a blur, the next station approaching in the distance. The letter remains in the bag, its words waiting patiently, unspoken. There is still time to read it, so I leave it inside the backpack. And I let the burden of it rest beside all the others. But it is not just Austin's burden I carry now, it is the echo of every voice silenced beneath certainty. I close my eyes and think of those I have known, those whose lives were marked by burdens heavier than mine.

There was a man, Osman from Sudan, who came into the church, his shoulders rounded by loss. He carried it like a second skin, like an inheritance he could not refuse. His wife, Zainab, a journalist, and their children fled for fear of death. They had left family behind, many were killed in the conflict-ridden region. When they arrived in the city, they were given shelter but not belonging. He sat in the pew, quiet, present but distant, as though some part of him had never truly arrived. They had escaped war, left behind everything they had ever known. His country was no longer his.

The home he had been born into, the land his ancestors had tilled and built, the streets he once walked without fear—all of it had been swallowed by conflict, by violence, by the kind of loss that takes more than lives. It takes belonging. It takes history.

On their treacherous journey, his young son was detained in Germany. He and his wife had found refuge in England, while their daughter had been sent on to Wales. Their asylum claim was refused. And that very week, they learned their son had died. "Why?"

Why does suffering come where love should have flourished? Why do the faithful still bleed?

Why does God, who split the sea, who called Lazarus from the grave, not intervene when the innocent fall?

I had no answer that would satisfy. No theology could sew up the wound left in his heart.

And yet, I sat with him. Sometimes, that is all we can do. Sometimes, faith is not the power to change things. It is the will to remain when nothing seems to change.

The train moves steadily forward, landscapes slipping past the window in a blur of motion and colour. I watch them without truly seeing. How many others on this train carry burdens unseen? How many move through the world with invisible scars, wounds that still ache though the bleeding has stopped? Survival is not the absence of wounds. Victory is not the absence of suffering. I can still feel the ache of the duffel bag as if it were still on my shoulder, the way the strap pressed into skin already too sensitive to strain. I tell myself it is just the fatigue of travel. But I know better. I know the deeper load—the one that no amount of rest can relieve.

It is the burden of years.

It is the residue of having walked through fire and knowing you still smell of the smoke.

I do not know how long Osman sat there praying, or how many prayers he had already prayed at home. I did not know how an asylum seeker buries a child who has died in a third country, or how to face that kind of loss. But I do know that he and his wife continued to have strong faith.

Faith is not always easy. It is not always the joyful thing we sometimes make it out to be in sermons and songs. Sometimes, faith is heavy. Sometimes, faith is the heft of the prayer that seems to have gone unanswered. Sometimes, faith is the burden of continuing to believe when the evidence of suffering presses too close, too deep, too relentlessly.

I think of my own prayers. I think of the nights I have pleaded—not for survival, for that has already been given—but for relief from the affliction that survival has left behind. There are days when I wonder if prayer itself is an act of endurance, a way of holding onto God even when the answers do not come in the way I had hoped. And if that is the case, then perhaps faith is not about receiving. Perhaps faith is about continuing to carry the burden, even when we do not understand it.

The train rattles on. The city is still far ahead. I watch the people around me. Some are reading, some are speaking in hushed voices, others stare out the window, lost in thought. What burdens do they carry? What griefs, what fears, what struggles sit heavy in their bones? I imagine them. The man near the door, dressed in a suit, his fingers tapping absently against the armrest—perhaps he carries the burden of a job that demands too much and gives too little. The woman two seats ahead, rubbing her temples as if warding off a headache—perhaps she carries the strain of a love that has faded, or a child she can no longer reach. The teenager scrolling through a phone, earbuds drowning out the world—perhaps they carry the weight of loneliness, of not yet knowing where they belong. We are all carrying something. Some burdens are seen. Others are silent. But all of them matter.

I think again of Osman and his family, how they fled war and lost a son. How Osman prayed a prolonged prayer, and when that became too heavy, he simply sat in the presence of God. Prayer is not always asking. Sometimes, prayer is simply existing in God's presence. Sometimes, it is breathing. Sometimes, it is just being still.

The train begins to slow as we approach another station. The doors open. People shuffle in and out. And I wonder, how many of them are carrying the burden of prayers they can no longer say? How many of them are still asking? How many of them have stopped asking because they are afraid to be met with silence? And yet, here we all are. Moving forward. Still breathing. Still carrying our burdens. Still holding onto something. Perhaps, in the end, faith is not about being unburdened. Perhaps faith is the willingness to keep walking, even when the burden remains.

The train moves again, pushing forward into the unknown. And I sit, watching the world slip past, breathing in measured sips, feeling the heaviness of all that I carry—not in my hands, but in my spirit. The burden remains. But so do I.

Breathing in the Past

10:30 AM

A cough rises in my throat, unbidden, and I suppress it as best I can. It is a cruel thing to survive a war and still feel the echoes of battle long after the fighting has ended. The cancer is gone, but it has left its mark. My lung is a stubborn thing, reluctant to stretch, tight as a clenched fist inside my chest.

And yet, I breathe.

Not always easily.

Not always fully.

But I breathe.

It is enough. Or at least that is what I tell myself. And I think of family who fought a good fight, never lost faith but no longer breathe. I know they have been gathered up. Gathered up to God's love and the love of our ancestors. As one day we will all be gathered.

The train rocks gently as it moves forward, the rhythm steady, the motion lulling the other passengers into the quiet lull of travel. Some doze against the windows, others flick through books or scroll through their phones. The world beyond the glass stretches out in long fields, houses clustered in the distance, roads curving like veins across the landscape, and I feel it, memory, pressing in, as constant as breath. Some pains fade with time. Others remain, woven into the fabric of the body itself.

The letter is still inside the backpack, folded neatly, waiting. I should continue reading it, but I prefer to let it rest. Yet something about its presence gnaws at me. A colleague in trouble, trouble of his own making. And though I delay, though I pretend the weight of it can be forgotten, I know the moment is coming, the moment when the truth will demand to be faced. I take the letter out, but I do not open it, not fully, not at first. Then I relent, my eyes find the next lines, just beyond what I had read before. He says,

"You've heard, I'm sure. Everyone has. There's no hiding from it anymore. The process is underway, the machine grinding forward as it always does. I have sat in rooms where men decided the fate of others, spoken words I thought were wise, nodded in agreement when judgment was passed. I knew the order of things. I believed in it."

I exhale, a slow, measured breath, and close my eyes for a moment. The train continues forward, steady. My hands tighten around the paper.

"The machine grinds forward," he says in the letter. The burden of decisions, of fates sealed in closed rooms, presses against the words I have just read. Austin, the man who wrote this—I thought I knew his character, I thought I knew who he was before he became someone condemned. What had he done? And more than that—what had he believed?

The past is not something we leave behind. It lingers in the body, in the breath, in the stories left unfinished. I am not sure if I am reading his confession—or holding my own indictment. And I wonder if, when the machine of judgment turned toward him, he finally understood what it meant to be on the other side. I sit with my hands clasped in my lap, the letter firm in my grip, my breath measured, feeling the pull of memory. Once, Austin was the one who weighed the "sins" of others. Once, he sat in a room where the fates of others were decided, where silence was demanded, where judgments were rendered in the cool, careful language of bureaucracy. A measured voice. A steady hand. A man of discernment, they called him. A man of faith.

And now?

Now, the machine he once served has turned toward him. Now, the ink stains his name. Now, he writes to me, not in authority, not in certainty, but in exile.

"You've heard, I'm sure. Everyone has," he says. Yes, I have heard. The whispers move like wind through the corridors of our world, through the sanctuaries where we once stood side by side. The ones who once trusted him now speak his name in hushed tones, careful, laden, as if it carries the power to stain. And I wonder, when he sat in judgment, when he peered across the table at those who had fallen, did he ever imagine himself in their place? Did he ever consider that one day, it would be his name on their lips, his file passed from hand to hand, his own sins laid bare for others to weigh? I do not know the details yet. Not fully. Only fragments, rumours that shift with each retelling. But guilt is not a question. That has already been established. The verdict is rendered. The judgment has passed. He has crossed the line, the same line he once held others to, and now he is the one waiting to see what remains of him after the fire. And yet, he writes to me. Not to protest. Not to deny. But why? What does he want from me, absolution, understanding? A witness to his fall, just as he was once a witness to the falls of others? Or is this something else entirely? A confession, maybe, or simply a voice crying out into the silence, hoping someone, anyone, will still listen?

There is an unease settling in my chest, something deeper than breathlessness, heavier than the burden of my own body. The letter is in my hands, but it is not just his story that unsettles me. It is the echoes of all those he once judged. What of them? The ones whose names we pretend we no longer remember, whose failures were dissected in closed rooms, whose lives were decided by people like him—they are the ones who haunt us. Were they given grace? Were they given mercy? Were they allowed to explain, to beg, to breathe before the sentence was pronounced? Or did he speak their fate with the same certainty that now seals his own? And if he showed no mercy, what right do I have to offer it now? Or was he too lenient? Too quick to overlook the harm that was done? Too quick to err on the side of the accused? And does he regret his decisions now? Does that matter? The past is not a thing that simply dissolves. It lingers. It clings. It waits. He has written to me. But I do not yet know if I will answer.

"I knew the order of things. I believed in it. Until it was me," he writes. Did he not believe in it now because he had been implicated? Or has he now realised that suffering is not just a philosophical dilemma but a human one? A reality that crushes, that unravels, that does not offer easy resolutions.

I think of his wife. She was always quiet, always present, but never loud in her devotion. She was not a woman who stood at the front of the church with grand proclamations. She was not the one others turned to for guidance, for deep theological discussions. She was simply there. A presence at Austin's side. And yet, how much did she truly know? Did she hear the whispers before the scandal broke? Did she sense the way Austin moved in certain rooms, the moments when his attention lingered in places it should not? Or was she, like the rest of us, simply trusting? And trust, once broken, leaves a wound deeper than betrayal itself. I do not know what it is like to be a wife watching her husband unravel. But I wonder if she is looking back now, trying to trace the steps that led here, just as I am.

And then there is the woman. The one spoken of now as though she is only that, a woman, a scandal, a name whispered but never fully voiced. I do not know her well. I never did. But I saw her. I saw the way she moved in the congregation, the way she carried herself, the way people spoke of her in admiration before they spoke of her in judgment. And I remember a night, a revival, when Austin was at the pulpit, and I looked across the room and saw him looking at her. It was not the look of a shepherd regarding his flock. It was something else. Something that, in hindsight, I wish I had acknowledged. Something that, perhaps, I did acknowledge and then chose to ignore. Because memory bends to protect us. And sometimes, protection feels easier than truth.

And then there are the children. Children do not have the luxury of bending memory. The children of the church saw. They walked into a space they should not have entered, and they saw. And now they will carry that moment with them. I wonder if Austin has thought of them. Not the whispers in the congregation, not the disciplinary meetings, not the formalities of judgment.

But the children.

The ones who once looked up at him with the unquestioning faith of the young. The ones who, in a single moment, had their trust severed, their understanding of truth shattered. They will carry this wound, invisible to the eye, but real all the same. And that is what stays with me. Not the council meetings, nor the formal letters of condemnation. But them.

And I wonder if that is what Austin means when he writes:

"I won't ask for sympathy. I won't even ask for understanding. I only ask this, when they speak my name, when they tally my failures, let there be one among you who remembers that I was not always this." I close the letter. I fold it carefully, pressing the creases down as if that might smooth something in me. I press it flat as if that could silence the questions it carries. My fingers linger on the paper's edges, tracing the gravity of words unspoken. He had once sat in judgment of others. Now, judgment has found him. And what is judgment, really, but the terrifying moment when your fate is no longer in your own hands?

That is the thought that takes me back. To the quiet tyranny of hospital rooms. To the sterile scent of disinfectant, pain, and sorrow. To the long hours spent waiting for verdicts I could not control. To the corridors lined with doors, each one leading to a room filled with hopes and fears, the hum of machines, the burden of prayers spoken in whispers. To sitting in comfortable chairs with chemicals slowly drip, dripping into my arm—potent poisons, designed to kill, chemical agents of death, administered for healing. Medicine that wounds in order to mend.

Nurses moving quietly, their footsteps purposeful, their hands cool against my skin as they adjusted IV lines, checked vitals, asked me to describe my pain on a scale of one to ten. Doctors speaking in measured tones, their voices careful, calculated, never betraying too much hope, never surrendering too much despair.

And my wife, Paige, who did not leave my side. She was there, through it all. She was the one who sat beside me, her hand firm in mine, her voice steady even when I knew she was afraid. She did not weep in front of me. If she did, it was in private, away from the beeping of the monitors, away from my weakened body, away from the hospital bed that had become our temporary world. She carried me, not in body, but in spirit. She spoke hope when I struggled to hold on to it. She prayed when I could not find the words. She bore witness to every moment, to every pain, to every flicker of healing that seemed to come too slowly. I do not know how she carried so much. And yet, she did. Because love carries. Because love does not turn away. Because love stays, even when the road ahead is uncertain.

And my mother. She came as soon as she could, traveling thousands of miles to spend time with us, with our family, with the life that I was fighting to keep. Though she did not sit at my bedside night after night, she was present. She knew I had survived. She lived to see the battle won. And that, perhaps, is the quiet grace in all of this. She did not have to wait in agony, wondering if her child would live or die. She did not have to bargain with God for more time. She saw me make it through. She knew I had overcome. She knew that my faith had not wavered. She knew that I had been given more years, more breath, more time. She saw my healing. She witnessed the answer to her prayers.

And yet, now—now she is gone. Gathered up to the love of God. Grief is a strange thing. I do not grieve her presence in my suffering, I had that. I grieve her absence in my survival. I grieve the years she has not seen, the moments she has not shared, the times I have reached for the phone to tell her something before remembering there is no number to call. Time has passed since she died. Since I last heard her voice. Since I could sit across from her, watch her expression change as we spoke, listen to the cadence of her speech, familiar, comforting, a sound that was part of the very fabric of my life. I want to tell her that I am still here. That I am still breathing, even when it is difficult. That I have not stopped believing, even when healing has not come in the way I hoped. That the breath I take now is still touched by the prayers she once prayed.

The train moves forward, and I think about all the breaths that have come before mine. The ones Paige waited for. The ones my mother gave thanks for. The ones that came in short, painful bursts when my body was still fighting to stay alive. And the ones that have continued long after she is gone. I shift in my seat, stretching my fingers, feeling the ache in my chest but refusing to be consumed by it. She is gone. And yet, she is not. Because she knew. Because she witnessed. Because she saw me through the storm and into the years beyond it. And because the breath I take now, though it is sometimes heavy, though it is sometimes hard, is still part of the life she prayed over, the life Paige fought beside me to keep. There is a strange thing that happens when you live through suffering: the past does not stay in the past. It lingers, weaving itself into the present, pressing into moments when you least expect it. It is in the way my fingers sometimes brush against my ribs, tracing the places where my body still remembers. It is in the way my breath catches on certain mornings, the way my lungs protest, the way my body whispers that survival does not always mean restoration. It is in the memory of Paige's hand in mine, steady and unwavering. It is in the absence of my mother's voice, in the space where she once was. And it is in the quiet knowing that I was loved through it all. This is the burden of memory, of love, and of survival I carry, but for me, there is an unknown burden to this letter.

The letter, much like my past suffering, carries a heaviness I am hesitant to face. Just as my body remembers pain and breath does not always come easily, the words within the letter might bring a different kind of suffocation—the kind that comes with knowing, with responsibility, with judgment. I have fought battles before, battles of body and spirit, with Paige at my side and my mother witnessing my survival. Their presence anchored me, gave me strength when I was at my weakest. But this letter? This letter is different. It does not carry love. It carries something else, something unfinished, something uncertain. It is not a hand gripping mine through the shadows of night, nor a prayer whispered to God seeking life. It is a reckoning, one I am not yet sure I want to face. Paige's love carried me, stayed through the worst of it, unwavering. My mother's faith bore witness to my survival, to the breath I still take now. But the letter carries no such promise. It does not offer the comfort of love or the reassurance of prayers answered. It is something else entirely, a door I am reluctant to open, just as breath does not always come freely. And so, I hesitate. Because to open it fully is to step into another kind of reckoning. And I am not sure I am ready to bear its load. Not yet.

The train begins to slow as we approach another station. The doors open. People shuffle in and out. And I wonder, how many of them carry absences as heavy as mine? How many have lost the ones who prayed for them? How many of them still feel the burden of hands that once held theirs, of voices they can no longer hear? How many of them carry the echoes of love that endured, even in suffering?

I take another breath.

Not deeply.

Not fully.

But enough.

Because Paige is still here.

Because my mother knew I survived.

Because the love that carried me still carries me now.

And because, I am still breathing.

When God Is Silent

11:00 AM

I have sat with pain before. I have held its trembling hands, looked into its hollowed-out eyes, listened to the sound of breath caught between sorrow and silence. But nothing prepares you for the burden of a question like this.

"Why would God allow that to happen to a little child?"

The words came from a woman barely past childhood herself. She sat across from me, arms crossed, her shoulders drawn inward, as though bracing for impact. Natalia had come seeking answers. But I knew already—there were no answers that could make what she had endured make sense. Her father was dead. A man she had fled across borders to escape. A man who had been more monster than blood, who had taken what he had no right to claim, left wounds that would not close. And now, she was here, not to grieve, but to wrestle with something deeper, something heavier

"Why would God allow that?"

I did not answer right away. Because before I could even think of what to say, another question came to mind—was I even the right person to answer? She was a young white woman. And I, a man, a Black man, a minister, someone shaped by struggles she had likely never known, sat across from her with the uncomfortable awareness that I might not be the person she needed to be speaking to. She had been hurt by a man. And here I was—another man. Would she trust me? Would she see me as someone who could understand? Or was there a barrier between us, one too large for this conversation to cross? Would she have been better off, and more comfortable speaking to a woman? Might a woman better carry the kind of embodied understanding that was needed? I did not know. But she had come to me. And I could not turn away.

What makes a minister worthy of trust? Shared belief, or shared wounds? Some questions are too large for words, too jagged to smooth over with comfort or rehearsed scripture. I could have said what others have said before—that suffering is a mystery, that we cannot know the mind of God, that evil exists because we have free will. But none of those words could touch the raw place inside her, the one that had been bleeding since she was a child. So I sat with her in silence. Because sometimes, silence is the only thing honest enough to hold suffering.

I thought of Job. A man who was righteous, a man who did everything right, and still, he lost everything. His children. His wealth. His health. His body, covered in sores. His friends, accusing him of sin. His wife, telling him to curse God and die. And Job, in the ashes, scraping his wounds with broken pottery, crying out to the heavens:

"Why?"

"I have done no wrong, why has this come upon me?"

But the answers did not come right away. Job did not receive an explanation. He received God's presence. God spoke, but not with reasons, not with justifications, not with a neatly wrapped theology that could soothe the rawness of his grief. Instead, God reminded Job of creation:

"Where were you when I laid the foundation of the earth? Tell me, if you have understanding."

In this, God was saying to Job: It is God alone who understands all things, including your suffering. It was not the answer Job had been seeking. But somehow, it was enough. Because sometimes it is not the answer that heals, but the awareness that God still speaks.

I thought of myself, of the nights I lay gasping for air, knowing I had survived but wondering why this body, this battered body, was what victory looked like. I thought of my mother's passing, how grief arrived as both an expected visitor and an unbearable stranger. I thought of my wife's hands, steady, unwavering, holding me when I was too weak to hold myself. And I thought of this young woman before me, who had suffered things no child should ever suffer, who now sat with eyes heavy from carrying questions that had no answers. She looked at me, waiting, pleading. And I knew she did not want theology. She did not want doctrine. She wanted justice. She wanted retribution. She wanted to know why the God who split seas, who raised the dead, had turned away when she was just a child. And what could I say? That God was silent? That God was there, but did nothing? That we live in a world where even children are not spared the cruelty of humanity?

I hesitated.

Not because I did not care. Not because I did not want to help. But because I did not know if I could. I was a stranger to her suffering. But I understood.

"I don't know why."

The words felt like failure. But they were the truth.

"I don't know why God allowed it. I don't know why some are born into love and others into war. I don't know why the ones who should protect us sometimes become the ones who break us."

Her eyes filled with tears. And she looked down to the floor.

"What I do know," I said, my voice steady, "is that God did not leave you there. You are here. You ran. You survived. And that is no small thing."

What I thought I saw was her nodding, just slightly, just enough. And it seemed to me, that she wept. Because sometimes the only answer to suffering is to acknowledge that it is real. That it is unfair. That it should not have happened. And yet, that survival is a kind of grace. A cruel, beautiful, defiant grace.

The train moves steadily beneath me, and I watch the world blur past. I unfurl the letter in my grip and regard the handwriting. Of course it is familiar, I have seen it on notes before passed to me by my colleague. But this time, the heft of the words feels like something foreign. A confession. A reckoning. I read:

"I knew the order of things. I believed in it. Until it was me."

Did he now not believe in it because he has been implicated? Has he now realized that suffering is not just a philosophical dilemma but a lived reality? Did he, too, now understand that sin isn't always abstract, and that theology cannot heal what you yourself have broken? Regarding his actions, does he now recognize why some ask the question,

"Why would God allow that?"

Is he facing the same crisis after having violated another? Does he see that the suffering he caused collapses certainty, making past beliefs feel fragile when faced with unbearable pain? He writes,

"I won't ask for sympathy."

I am certain that there is a difficulty in finding comfort or absolution in suffering, when you have been the cause of the suffering. Just as Natalia did not want doctrine or theology, my colleague is not seeking an easy answer. And he shouldn't, he has caused harm when he should have been a trusted, safe pair of hands.

Both Natalia and my colleague are burdened by what has been done, one burdened by the actions of another and the other burdened by their actions, by the brutal realities of the world. I find that there is a stark recognition that pain cannot be undone, that suffering does not always lead to justice. I do not have answers. But I have presence. I have breath. I have faith, not because it has been easy, but because it has endured. Because if suffering is real, then so is the One who does not turn away from it. And if the world is broken, then faith is not naïveté—it is resistance.

I think about suffering, not just the suffering of one, but the suffering of all. The child born into famine, their ribs pressing against thin skin. The mother burying her child son, another name lost to war. The father watching his family slip further into poverty, his hands calloused from labor that will never be enough. The body that survived cancer but still fights to breathe. And all of them, in their own way, asking the same questions:

"Why?"

"How much longer?"

There was another man, long after Job, who cried out with the same question. Not in the ashes, but on a cross. Not in words of poetry, but in agony.

"My God, my God, why have You forsaken me?"

Even The Word, even The One who was with God from the beginning, even The One who healed the sick and raised the dead—even He asked the question.

"Why?"

And there was no answer. Not in that moment. Only suffering. Only silence. And then, resurrection. But resurrection is not reversal. Resurrection is not the erasure of pain, nor the undoing of wounds. The nails left scars. The spear left its mark. Even in glory, the wounds remained. And so we who bear the burden of suffering, we who cry out from hospital rooms and grieving pews, from war-torn borders and empty kitchen tables, we who ask "Why?" and receive no answer, we are not alone. For The One who cried out still carries the scars. For The One who was forsaken is now The One who walks beside us. For the silence of God is not the absence of God. And though we wait, though the suffering lingers, though the world groans for redemption, resurrection still comes. Not always as we expect. Not always as we desire. But it comes. Not as reversal, but as presence. Not as an undoing, but as a going forward. Wounded, but alive. Scarred, but risen.

The train hums beneath me, steady. I put Austin's letter away and look out the window, watching the light shift, the sky bending toward noon. I do not have answers. But I have presence. I have breath. I have faith, not because it has been easy, but because it has endured. I have seen suffering. I have carried it. But I have also seen love. I have seen the ones who run, survive, weep, and still believe. I do not know why suffering remains.

But I know this, God is not in the cruelty, God is in the ones who survive it, and God is in the ones who do not survive it, God's is the hand that holds the wounded, God is the presence that sits beside the silence, God is the love that lingers even when all else is lost. Because if suffering is real, then so is The One who does not turn away from it. The One who walks through fire and famine, war and weeping, shadow and silence. The One who was there, even when the night was at its deepest. The One who remained, even when all seemed forsaken. God is in the breath that still draws. God is in the ones who carry the questions and still choose to love. God is in the ones who do not make it through, because they are not lost. Because the hands that made the stars are the hands that hold the broken. And because they are held, I will keep holding, too. And not one of them, not one of us, is ever left behind.

Beneath the Ash

11:30 AM

The train is steady beneath me, the hum of motion a quiet comfort. I rest my head against the cool glass of the window, feeling the vibration of the journey in my bones. The rhythm of movement carries me forward, but my mind drifts backward, circling the same questions I've carried for years. I have seen faith hold steady in the face of unimaginable loss. And I have seen it slip through fingers like sand, lost to the burden of suffering. Some people endure hardship and cling tighter to God, as if faith is the only anchor in a storm that will not pass. Others let go, their hands emptied by grief, unable to believe in a God who would allow such pain. I have watched both kinds of people. And I have wondered what makes the difference. What decides whether we rise or unravel? Is it belief? Or is it something far more fragile?

There was a woman in my congregation, faithful, devoted, never missed a Sunday. She sat in the same pew every week, sang the hymns with reverence, bowed her head in prayer with quiet intensity. And yet, one day, she stopped coming. Not because of her own pain, but because she saw it in others. Her friends, a good and faithful couple, who were also members of the church, suffered loss after loss. Their son-in-law was sick. Their own health was failing. Then, the family suffered a sudden death, what seemed like an unexpected cruelty when they were already burdened by so much. With each blow, she watched them stagger, watched them struggle, watched their faith, once so certain, tested in ways she had never seen before. While they endured, for her that was enough. Enough for her to decide that faith, this thing she had held onto for so long, no longer made sense. That a just God would not allow the faithful to suffer so greatly. That belief had to be exchanged for something else, perhaps bitterness, perhaps nothingness. I watched her walk away from the altar, and when I tried to speak, the words would not come. Not because I did not care, but because I had no answer to offer, only the same aching questions she carried with her. She did not hate God. She simply no longer saw God. And I had no words to rekindle her faith. She no longer believed God could be good.

Faith and belief—they are not the same thing. Belief is what we think. Faith is what we live. And when belief crumbles, faith does not always survive the fall. That is what I am learning, that faith is more than mental assent. It is more than doctrine or dogma or the repetition of creeds. It is something deeper, quieter, harder to define. Something that persists even when belief falters. When I was gasping for breath, faith was not in my theology—it was in my wife's hand holding mine through the night. I think often about the relationship between faith and belief. Belief is something we construct, statements, affirmations, ideas we hold as true. It can be taught, debated, even proven or disproven in our minds. But faith is something else entirely. Faith is trust without condition. It is the act of holding on when belief has no logical ground to stand on. Faith lives in the space where certainty has failed.

Austin's letter lingers in my mind.

"Let there be one among you who remembers: I was not always this."

And I do remember. I remember a man who stood beside me at services, who spoke words of wisdom, who once believed in the order of things. A man whose sermons stirred hearts, whose prayers carried significance. But I also remember a man who let himself be drawn into something that unraveled him, who sat in judgment of others while concealing his own guilt, who has now written to me in the remnants of his disgrace. Did he still believe?

Did he pray? Or had faith slipped through his fingers, lost beneath the gravity of consequence?

"I don't know why I'm writing. Maybe because there's no one left to listen. Maybe because silence has never suited me, and yet now it is all I have."

The silence of exile. That is what he now lives with. Austin, who once spoke so assuredly of God's justice, now wonders if anyone will remember him beyond his worst moment. Perhaps the woman in my congregation and Austin are not so different. One abandoned faith because she saw others suffer unjustly. The other abandoned righteousness and now suffers because of his own failings. Both have been emptied. Both have been left in the silence. And perhaps both still long for something, perhaps not the certainty of belief, but the comfort of faith. Perhaps faith, when stripped of its language, rituals, and theology, is simply the refusal to let go completely.

Across the world, in the aftermath of an earthquake, there was another woman. A woman who had lost everything, home, family, a life she had built and loved. She was buried beneath the debris, alone in the wreckage, waiting for death. And when they found her, when the hands of strangers pulled her from the ruins, from the tomb that had nearly claimed her, we did not see her weep for what was lost. She did not curse God for the ruin around her. Instead, she lifted her voice in praise.

Two women; two lives marked by suffering. One turned away, the other turned toward.

Why?

I do not pretend to have the answer. But I know this, that faith is not a thing measured by logic. It is not a transaction, where goodness ensures prosperity and hardship means betrayal. It is not a shield that protects against suffering. Faith is something else entirely. It is what remains when all else is lost.

I think of my ancestors. They were bound, shackled, crammed into the bowed cruelty of ships that carried them across the Atlantic, away from their names, their families, their language, their freedom. They lived under the lash, their backs bearing the scars of a world that refused to see their humanity. Their children were born into chains, they lived in chains, they died in chains. And yet, somehow, their faith remained. They stood on auction blocks and whispered the name of God. They labored under the sun, hands raw from work not of their choosing, and still they lifted their voices in songs of deliverance. They knelt in fields, in hidden places, in hush harbors where no oppressor could hear, and they prayed.

They prayed. Not because they had reason to believe the world would suddenly be just. Not because their suffering would be erased. But because faith was the only thing that could not be stolen, could not be sold, could not be beaten out of them. Their faith survived because it was not rooted in outcomes, it was rooted in presence. In the nearness of God, even when the world was far from just. And so, I ask myself: Where does faith come from? Why does it endure in some and wither in others? Perhaps faith remains not because we choose it, but because something in us is awakened by The One who will not let go. Because somewhere deep in the soul, there is a flame that refuses to be snuffed out, even when the winds of life howl against it.

Perhaps faith is not about whether we suffer, but about whether we believe suffering has the final word. Perhaps the woman who turned from God saw suffering as proof that she had been abandoned. And perhaps the woman pulled from the rubble saw suffering as proof that she was still here. That breath itself was a gift. That survival was an answer, even if it was not the answer she had wanted. And perhaps my ancestors knew something, something that stretches across generations, across oceans, across the wreckage of time. That even when all else is lost, faith can remain. That even when the body is broken, the spirit does not have to be. That God was never in the chains. God was in the breaking of them. And perhaps Austin's silence is not absence of faith, but the beginning of its return. Maybe the letter itself is a prayer, unspoken, uncertain, but still reaching.

The train moves forward, but my mind moves backward. Austin.

I turn his name over in my mind, weighing it. He once believed suffering was a test of faith, a measure of one's endurance. He once spoke of righteousness as though it was something one could hold on to, unshaken. And now? Now, judgment has come for him. Now, he sits in silence, waiting for the verdict. I wonder if he sees himself as forsaken. I wonder if he prays, not for redemption, but simply for something, anything, to remain.

"P.S. I am still here. But for how much longer, I cannot say."

To be "still here" is perhaps all that faith requires. Not certainty. Not perfection. Just the refusal to vanish completely. I think about those words often.

Still here.

Faith, I have come to believe, is not a triumphant march but a quiet standing. A decision to remain rooted even when the ground feels uncertain. It is the choice to rise, even after the fall. The decision to speak, even when no one seems to listen. The willingness to hope, even when every visible sign suggests despair.

The train continues forward, each mile taking me closer to my destination. But my thoughts are elsewhere. I think about my own faith. How it has stretched, shifted, changed shape over the years. How it has survived sickness, grief, loss. How it has remained, even when the questions were too heavy, even when the silence was too long, even when the breath was too short.

There was a night during my illness when I nearly let go. Not of life. But of faith. The pain had been relentless, the exhaustion deeper than anything I had ever known. My prayers felt like echoes in an empty room. And I thought, what if faith is just another thing that will fail me? I did not say it aloud. But God heard it anyway. And there was no great revelation that night. No miracle. No voice speaking from the heavens, no sudden ease of suffering. But there was presence. There was breath. I woke the next morning.

Still weary.

Still wounded.

Still wondering.

And somehow, still believing. As if faith itself had held me when I could not hold it.

I am still here. And as long as I am, I will not let silence be the last word. Not for Austin. Not for me. Not for the faith that refuses to die.

The train slows as we approach another station. People gather their belongings, shuffle toward the doors, step onto the platform. And I wonder, how many of them carry faith? How many have lost it? How many are trying to decide whether to hold on or let go?

Faith is not an easy thing. It does not always make sense. But I have learned this: Faith is not in the answers. Faith is in the endurance. Faith is what remains.

The Hands of the Clock, the Hands of God

12:00 PM

The train moves forward, steady, unrelenting. The rhythm of the wheels against the tracks is a whisper, a metronome marking the passage of time. I close my eyes for a moment, feeling the burden of it, not just the heft of the bag at my feet or the breathlessness in my chest, but the gravity of time itself. Time moves whether we are ready or not. It pulls us forward even when we wish to stay still. It carries us into the future, whether we welcome it or fear it. And I have always been aware of time, not just because of my own body, the way it marks survival in years since remission, in decades beyond diagnosis, but because time has always been something I have felt pressed upon me.

Austin's letter sits in my bag, its presence a quiet, inescapable thing. He, too, is aware of time now. Not in the way I am, not in the counting of breaths given, in the unexpected grace of years that were once uncertain, but in the way that comes when time is running out.

"I don't know why I'm writing. Maybe because there's no one left to listen. Maybe because silence has never suited me, and yet now it is all I have."

Time has carried him into exile. He once believed in its certainty, in the steady rhythm of righteousness. But now, he is unmoored. Now, he is the one sitting in the silence, waiting for judgment to pass.

"I have sat in those rooms before, where judgment is passed, spoken words I thought were wise, nodded in agreement and called it justice."

Time is not measured in hours for him now. It is measured in the waiting. In the space between disgrace and whatever comes next. And what does come next, for him? For me? For the ones left holding the consequences of what he has done?

I think of my mother. She was a woman who was not pressured by the urgency of time. She had a wooden board in her kitchen that read: The hurrier I go the behinder I get. She measured life not in clocks or calendars but in the lives of those she loved, in the time she could spend with them, in the moments that were given and the ones that were slipping away. I still hear her voice in the quiet, in the spaces between breaths. I still feel the presence of her prayers, lingering like echoes that refuse to fade. Time took her. And yet, somehow, love remains.

Austin's wife, I imagine, must feel the opposite. Time has not taken her husband, but it has taken everything else. Her place in the congregation. Her certainty in the life they had built together. Her name is not in the letter Austin sent me. And yet, she is there. Because judgment does not fall on one person alone, it drags down all who were near them. And what of her faith? Does she still pray for him? Or does she now pray for herself alone, for strength to carry what he left behind?

I shift in my seat, glancing at the clock above the train doors. The digital numbers flicker slightly as the train jolts over the tracks, marking the hour, the minute, the second. Time is measured in such precise ways now. But I think of the ways my ancestors measured time, not in numbers, but in survival. Their time was stolen. Their years were dictated by enslavers, by labor, by laws that sought to erase their existence. And yet, they reclaimed it. In hush harbors, whispering prayers. In songs that carried hope across fields. In stolen moments of rest, of breath, of faith. They understood time in a way I am only beginning to grasp. Not as something that belongs to the powerful, but as something sacred. Something that cannot truly be owned, only lived. And if I do not live that time well, then whose sacrifices have I squandered?

Austin believed in the authority of time once. He believed that he stood outside of judgment, that he was the one who measured others, that his position allowed him to decide what was righteous and what was not. And now, time has turned against him. Now, he is the one waiting for others to decide his fate.

"P.S. I am still here. But for how much longer, I cannot say."

I wonder how he counts the days now. I wonder if he wakes in the morning and feels the pressure of time pressing down on him, not the way my grandfather did, standing before his clock, watching the hands move forward, but in the way that comes when the future is no longer yours to shape.

There is a memory that stays with me, one I did not live but was given. A story passed down. It was about my grandfather. I never met him, he died before I was born. But the stories of him remain. He was a man of discipline, knowledge, and understanding. A man who believed that time was something to be honored. His respect for time came at an early age. When he was young, his parents gave him a gift.

A clock.

A tall standing clock, imbued with meaning. For them, it was not just a timepiece. It was a promise. A vision of something greater than the past they had endured. The clock pointed to the future. It was a proclamation that time did not belong only to those who had once owned their bodies. That their son's hours and days and years would not be dictated by the legacy of enslavement, but by his own ambition, his own will. It was a symbol of hope, of movement, of progress. It ticked not just seconds, but generations forward. To own time—to measure it, to mark it, to look toward it—was a powerful thing. Enslavement had stolen time from them. It dictated when they could wake, when they could work, when they could rest, and even when they could die. The clock was their way of reclaiming that power, of saying: No more. Now, we decide. And my grandfather, with that clock in his possession, carried forward their vision. He did not squander the hours they had fought to give him.

He studied.

He built.

He taught.

He poured into the next generation so that they, too, would understand that they were not bound by the past, but rather, lifted by it. I wonder if he ever felt the full gravity of it. And if he sat in the quiet and listened to its steady ticking, a sound that was likely both a comfort and a challenge. I wonder if he woke each morning and wound it with careful hands, the way one might tend to an altar, watching the hands move forward, watching the pendulum sway, the weights shifting in measured certainty. Did he stand before it, not merely checking the time, but witnessing it, acknowledging each second as something earned, something given, something that could never again be taken.

What will you do with the time you have been given? I think about my own time now, how fragile it feels, how each breath reminds me that survival is a borrowed thing. I think about how my body bears the battle scars of living, how I, too, have been given time that I did not expect to have. And I think about the responsibility of that. Because time is never just ours alone. It belongs to those who came before us, to those who fought and endured, those who dreamed beyond their own lifetimes. Time belongs to those who will come after us, who will look back and ask what we did with the hours we were given.

Austin did not tend to time the way my grandfather did. And maybe not many of us do. But Austin let the hours slip, let the burden of his authority convince him that he had time to spare, time to waste, time to hide behind the righteousness of his past words. And now?

Now, he has run out of it. Now, he writes to me, hoping for a different kind of time, the kind that comes with redemption. But redemption is not something I can give him. Only God can do that.

The train slows as we approach another station. And as the doors slide open, a new wave of passengers steps in. Some look at

35

their watches, their phones, checking the time, measuring their schedules against the movement of the train. I wonder how many of them think about time the way I have come to do. Or the way my mother or grandfather did. Not as something to rule their lives or to be managed, but as something to work with. Not as something we own, but as something we are given. Not as something to fear, but as something to honor. I look at the time again. Not the digital numbers above the door, but the time that exists beyond clocks. The time that lingers in memory. The time that remains in breath. The time that was fought for, prayed for, passed down. And I know, when I speak again, when I write back to Austin, if I write back, I will do so from that kind of time. And I know this, I will not waste it. I will not take it for granted. I will not live as though my time is only my own.

The clock still ticks. The future still waits. And we should all decide how to spend the time we have been handed.

The Sound Between Words

The train moves, a steady hum beneath my feet, a rhythmic reminder of time pressing forward. The window frames a world in
motion, fields stretching beyond sight, trees bending slightly as if
whispering secrets to the wind. I watch them pass, each mile pulling me closer to the meeting, to the conversations waiting like a
storm at the horizon. This meeting will not be easy. These discussions, long avoided, long softened by those who feared discomfort,
will demand truth. The truth about harm. The truth about those
who have used sacred spaces as shields for their wrongdoing. The
truth about the suffering left in their wake. The truth about the
justice we, as church, must deliver for victims.

And Austin. He writes:

"I have sat in those rooms before, where judgment is passed,
spoken words I thought were wise, nodded in agreement and
called it justice."

Now, Austin is the one waiting for judgment. And I wonder,
did he ever think this reckoning would come for him? And when it
did come, did he imagine it would arrive not like thunder, but like
a whisper passed between ministers in the hallway, or a letter slid
quietly across a table? It is easier to speak of grace than to speak
of justice. Easier to offer prayers than to demand accountability.
Easier to turn away, to let time settle over wounds, hoping that
silence will be enough to heal what has been broken. But silence
has never healed anything.

I press my hand against my chest, feeling the steady beat beneath my ribs. The body remembers what words try to forget. The ones who have been harmed, do they not carry the burden of it in their bodies, in their breaths, in the sleepless nights where the past refuses to stay buried? And what of the others? The families who have been fractured by betrayal? The ones who sit in pews, who bow their heads in reverence, all while wondering if the place they once called safe was ever truly safe at all? This is the load we carry. Not just the harm itself, but the consequences rippling outward, reaching those who were never meant to bear them. And I am not immune. I have been in rooms where I should have said more. Rooms where my silence protected the institution, not the broken. This is what I will face when I step into that meeting. And I wonder, will they be ready to see? Will they be ready to look at what we have ignored for too long? Because to see means to name it. And to name it means to acknowledge that faith has been misused, that power has been wielded like a weapon, that some have stood on pulpits and spoken of love while leaving destruction in their path. I close my eyes, the train's motion still steady beneath me. I think of Austin. I think of his voice in those meetings, speaking with certainty, with authority, with the unwavering conviction that justice must be done.

"We must be unwavering." he said, "Sin must be met with consequence."

And now, he is the one waiting for consequence. Did he think, then, that he would ever sit in this silence? That one day, it would be his name spoken in careful, measured tones? That he would be the one stripped of his power, his reputation, his certainty? Austin judged others as though he himself would never be measured by the same standard. And now? Now, he has fallen. Now, he writes to me, asking to be remembered for more than his worst moment.

"Let there be one among you who remembers: I was not always this."

But what does it mean to remember? Does it mean to erase what has been done? Or does it mean to hold it all—the good and the ruin—in equal measure?

We like to believe we would do what is right. That, given the choice, we would not be the ones calling for the release of Barabbas—whose freedom the crowd demanded while Jesus was sentenced to death—or be the ones washing our hands, as Pilate did, pretending to absolve ourselves while injustice unfolded before us. But the truth is, it is easier to look away than to confront what demands to be seen. Easier to soften our words, to speak of grace without justice, to speak of love without consequence. Easier to say,

"It was long ago."

"It is in the past."

"They have repented."

But what of those who were harmed? Does time erase wounds? Does repentance undo what has been broken? We have long misunderstood justice. We have imagined it as something separate from mercy, as though one cancels out the other. As though to hold someone accountable is to deny them grace. But the grace we can give does not come with the absence of accountability. But what is grace without truth? What is forgiveness without the full weight of what is being forgiven? Our grace is not the silencing of pain in the name of peace. The grace we can give is the presence of truth, the willingness to name what has been done, the courage to seek restoration—not through forgetting, but through facing what has been shattered. And yet, there are those who will resist. There are those who will say that to speak too openly is to weaken faith, to expose too much is to do more harm than good. But what harms faith more? The truth, or the burden of deception? The exposure of wrongdoing, or the silence that allows it to continue? We do not honor the sacred by shielding the corrupt. We do not protect faith by protecting those who have twisted it to serve themselves. Because the heart of our faith is not denial, but revelation. Not concealment, but incarnation.

And God,

God faces the suffering of the wounded and refuses to trade compassion for the preservation of power. And neither should we.

I close my eyes for a moment, feeling the motion of the train, the rhythm beneath me steadying my thoughts . . . the cross is more than sacrifice. It is a mirror. A mirror that reveals more than we wish to see. It shows us the ones who turned away. The ones who remained silent. The ones who justified their actions, who convinced themselves that what they allowed, what they ignored, what they permitted, was not their burden to bear. It shows us the ones who chose self-preservation over truth. And we are there, in the reflection. Not just in the failures of others, but in our own. We are the ones who looked away. The ones who justified silence. The ones who made excuses for those who wielded their position not to heal, but to harm. We do not like to see ourselves in these stories. We like to believe we would have done differently. But the cross tells the truth. And the truth is this: We have failed. Failed to listen when cries rose. Failed to act when the evidence was clear. Failed to choose what was right when it was easier to choose comfort. The gospel we proclaim must be able to withstand the truth we have tried to bury—if it cannot, then it is not good news. And yet—even in our failure, we are still seen. Even in our betrayal, grace does not abandon us. It is not because we deserve it or have done what is right, it is because God does not leave us to be defined by our worst moments. God sees the wounds we have caused and still offers a path to redemption. God's love does not turn away. Austin will face his judgment, and so will we. Not only for what we have done, but for what we have allowed. For what we have refused to see. And for the truths we have swallowed to make ourselves more comfortable. We as ministers are called to be shepherds, so let us begin by leading with truth. We are called to be healers, so let us begin with tending to wounds.

The train moves, the sky outside shifting, the light bending over the horizon. I think of the meeting ahead. The words that will be spoken. The words that must be spoken. I think of the ones who will resist. The ones who will say that we must be careful with how we speak. That we must protect reputations. That we must be mindful of how much truth we reveal. But truth does not destroy faith. Truth strengthens it. Truth is the foundation upon which all healing stands. If we do not speak honestly, if we do not name what has been broken, if we do not seek justice with the same fervor with which we speak of mercy, then what is our faith? A facade. A hollow thing. A structure built on avoidance, waiting to collapse beneath the strain of its own deception. That is not what we are called to. We are called to bear witness. To name what has been done. To refuse to allow silence to cover wounds that must be healed. And we must remember this: Healing is truth telling. Healing acknowledges the wound was real. Healing is carrying the scars and choosing to live anyway.

And from that healing, a deeper call emerges: the call to justice and mercy. They are companions. Each incomplete without the other. Justice and mercy must walk together, or they are neither. Because justice alone becomes something hard and unrecognizable. A cold pursuit of retribution without restoration. It names the wrong but forgets the heart that carried it. And mercy, when it stands apart from truth, becomes something weightless. A softness that excuses what must be confronted.

A kindness that smooths over harm but does not mend it. It speaks of grace but leaves the wound open, unacknowledged, unhealed. Justice names what has been broken.

Mercy refuses to discard the one who broke it. We are not called to choose between them, as though they are on opposite sides. We are called to hold them together—so that in naming the wound, we do not lose sight of the person. So that in offering grace, we do not abandon what is right. Justice and mercy must walk together. Because without that union, there is no wholeness. No restoration. No truth that sets free.

The train moves forward. And by grace, we move with it.

Words Born of Pain

1:00 PM

Healing does not always erase wounds. It allows us to live beyond them, to carry the burden of endurance with the grace of a God who does not avoid suffering but steps into it. And so I ask myself: is this why we gravitate toward the Word? Because it speaks in the language of affliction, because it understands what it means to be broken? Does the recognition of God with us, God who has suffered, help foster a closeness, a bond?

The train rumbles beneath me, steady but unyielding, a reminder that motion does not always mean progress. Across the aisle, a middle-aged man flips through a paperback novel, his face impassive. A few seats down, a young woman with headphones types away on a laptop, her fingers moving quickly as though chasing a fleeting thought. And then there's the catering steward, a short, sturdy man in a navy-blue uniform pushing a trolley filled with hot and cold drinks, sandwiches, and neatly wrapped pastries. The scent of fresh coffee and warmed croissants reaches me before he does, mingling with the scent of metal and movement. I don't buy anything, though the thought crosses my mind. Appetite has never been the same since illness, it comes and goes in waves, sometimes absent for hours, then suddenly, I am starving. Instead, I watch as he stops at each row, exchanging small talk, offering refreshments, moving forward. This moment, so mundane, so ordinary, is something I might have overlooked before. But there is something to be said about witnessing the everyday lives of others, about seeing people in moments unburdened by existential heaviness. I envy them. I envy their unknowing. I envy that they do not seem haunted by every breath, by the invisible weight of survival. I watch them—the man with his novel, the woman with her laptop, the steward with his trolley—and I am struck by how life goes on, how stories unfold around us, unnoticed. How every person carries a hidden narrative, a quiet ache or a private hope. Maybe that is why the Bible feels so alive to me: because it, too, is a record of lives interrupted, of ordinary people thrust into extraordinary suffering.

The Bible is a set of books born in discomfort. It is the product of lives marked by suffering—none untouched by pain. The Bible was written in exile, in slavery, in persecution. It was shaped by those who had seen their cities burn, their homes torn apart, their children taken. It was formed in the mouths of prophets who cried out in anguish, in the prayers of kings who knew both triumph and ruin, in the voices of disciples who watched their Messiah breathe His last. The Bible is not a book that avoids suffering—it is a book that emerges from it. And so I wonder: have we forgotten that? Is that why, for many, it feels so distant now? We have tried to scrub the blood from its pages. We have tried to turn lament into something polite.

Have we turned faith into a comfortable thing, something meant to soothe rather than convict? Something polished and respectable, rather than something born of struggle, born of survival against the odds? Have we forgotten that it is meant to offer hope where there seems to be none? The words still speak because they were written by the wounded, for the wounded. I sit with the thought. Austin, too, has been wounded. His letter remains in my bag, folded and unread beyond the words I have already let sink into my bones.

"I have sat in those rooms before, where judgment is passed, spoken words I thought were wise, nodded in agreement and called it justice."

Now, he is the one in exile. He is the one waiting for the burden of words to be spoken against him, waiting for the decision that will determine what remains of his life. But is exile enough? Is silence a fair reckoning for the wounds left bleeding in his wake? Does he see himself in the stories of scripture now? Does he feel a kinship with the fallen kings, with the exiled prophets, with those whose names became synonymous with failure? Or does he only feel the absence? The silence. The emptiness that follows when the world has turned away?

"I won't ask for sympathy. I won't even ask for understanding. I only ask this, when they speak my name, when they tally my failures, let there be one among you who remembers: I was not always this."

And I wonder, who remembers the woman? The one whose name is now a whisper, the one whose presence has been reduced to scandal. The one who, like so many before her, has been erased in the fallout of a man's disgrace. Justice is not remembering the fallen powerful. Justice is remembering the ones they forgot. Does Austin think of her? Or does his exile feel so total that he has forgotten that she, too, has been cast out?

But this isn't the first time exile has rewritten the story. This isn't the first time silence has threatened to erase someone's name. From the very beginning, the story of God's people begins in struggle and survival—where memory itself becomes an act of resistance. The Israelites were not a people unfamiliar with chains. First under Pharaoh, then under Babylon, and finally under Rome, their history was marked by captivity, by displacement, by the constant threat of erasure. And yet, in the midst of their suffering, they wrote. They remembered. They passed down the stories of deliverance, even as they waited for deliverance to come again. The Psalms are filled with lamentations, prayers of the afflicted, the broken, the weary.

"How long, O Lord? Will You forget me forever?" (Psalm 13:1).

"My tears have been my food day and night—" (Psalm 42:3).

"Do not hide Your face from me when I am in distress" (Psalm 102:2).

These are not words of a people who had never known suffering. These are the cries of those who have walked through fire. And yet, through the cries, there is faith. There is the unshaken, stubborn belief that God is still present in the midst of pain. I think of Job, sitting in the ashes of his own ruin, his body wrecked, his children lost, his name reduced to whispers of pity. And still, he did not stop speaking to God. Even when all he had left were questions. Even when all he had left was anger. And I wonder, how many of us carry that same kind of faith? The faith that refuses to let go, even when everything else has been taken? The Bible does not promise that pain will not come. It does not pretend that faith shields us from loss. Instead, it shows us what it means to hold on to God in the midst of it. To cry out in grief and still believe. To wrestle with doubt and still cling to hope. To be broken and still remain. And that is why the words still speak. Because we, too, know exile. We, too, have seen suffering. We, too, bear wounds, some visible, some carried deep within. And yet, like those before us, we write. We remember. We tell the story of survival. Because faith is profoundly held on to, in the midst of hardship. It was meant for the wounded, the weary, the ones who have walked through fire and still believe in something beyond the ashes. It is not doubt that kills faith. It is forgetting who we are in the ashes.

The journey continues. The train rattles forward, steady but unyielding. The steward moves down the aisle, stopping at each row, engaging in the simple, reverent act of serving. The young woman's fingers dance across the keyboard, capturing something fleeting yet important. The man with the paperback turns another page, lost in a world not his own. And I sit with my thoughts, with the gravity of history and faith pressing into me. The words still speak because they were written by the broken, for the broken. And as for me? I have been broken. But I am still here. And in every breath, in every memory, I am still writing my part of the story.

Breath Found in the Telling

1:30 PM

The train hums beneath me, steady and indifferent, as if unaware of what I carry in my hands. Austin's letter now lies open on my lap once again.

"I knew the order of things. I believed in it once."

The handwriting is slanted, slightly rushed, as though he was uncertain whether the words should be written at all. I've read and reread his words, and still, I find myself stuck on that line. Not just because of what he says—but because of what he doesn't. There's a tone beneath it. Not quite confession. Not quite defiance. Just the dull weight of someone who no longer believes in his own story. I fold the letter shut and let it rest on the tray table. My reflection stares back at me faintly in the window — blurry, shifting, fractured by the passing light.

Trauma leaves us unanchored. It tears us from what we thought we knew, from the safety we believed in, from the certainty that life would be fair. It shatters the illusion of control, leaving us raw, exposed, searching for something solid to hold firmly to. It teaches us, in the cruelest way, that not all hands are gentle, that not all promises are kept, that not all who are meant to protect us, will.

For some, the betrayal is singular—a moment, a breach, a collapsing of trust that happens all at once, an instance where trust is shattered. For others, it is an echo, reverberating through years, through decades, through lifetimes. It is a slow erosion, a steady dismantling of belief in the goodness of the world. The wounds inflicted by those we should have been able to trust—the guardians, the mentors, the family, the institutions meant to shelter us—cut deeper than most. They rewrite the very structure of our souls, leaving us questioning not only others but ourselves.

I have heard the echoes over time—quiet ones. Whispers that never reached the threshold of proof, but sat in the corner of rooms like something unspoken but known.

Rumors.

I heard them.

And I told myself that to hear was not the same as to know. But now, holding this letter, reading the sorrow woven through Austin's words, I wonder if that was a way to protect myself from what I feared was true.

And Austin.

He has left his own fractures.

"I knew the order of things. I believed in it once."

And now, those who once sat beside him, who once looked to him as a guide, are left reeling from his fall. The burden of his choices is not his alone to bear. It is carried by those who trusted him, by those who sat in the rooms where his voice once held authority.

And by the children.

By the ones who saw.

By the ones who will never see the world the same way again. Their innocence was not just stolen. It was shattered into something unrecognizable. There is no suffering too deep for God to understand. That is what I have always believed. But what of the suffering we cause each other? What of the wounds inflicted not by fate, but by choice? Yet, in that unraveling, some of us find refuge in the very thing that was born out of trauma itself. We find a home in the words of the Bible. Not because it offers easy answers—because it does not. It never claims that suffering will vanish, that justice will be immediate, that wounds will simply close without scars. No, the Bible does not lie to us about pain. It does not wrap suffering in platitudes or pretend that faith will erase what has been endured.

Instead, it speaks in the language of the brokenhearted. It meets us where we are, in the shadows, and it does not ask us to pretend the night is not real. It speaks because it was written in the shadows, for those still walking through it.

When we read the cries of David, the very cries Jesus later quoted on the cross—"My God, my God, why have You forsaken me?"—I know we hear the echo of our own voices. When we see Job sitting in the ashes, stripped of everything, questioning the justice of the world, we recognize the depth of our own grief. When we walk with the Israelites through the wilderness, lost and wandering, unsure of where God is leading, we understand what it means to carry doubt and faith in the same breath. And when we stand at the foot of the cross, watching Jesus—betrayed, beaten, abandoned—we see that God has known suffering. That God has stepped into it, felt its burden, borne its wounds. And so, I wonder—does Austin see himself in these stories now? Does he see himself in the fallen kings, the exiled prophets, the ones who misused what was given to them? Or does he see himself only as forsaken?

There is no suffering too deep for God to understand. Yet, understanding is not the same as healing. Knowing that suffering is seen does not undo its consequences. But God's understanding is not like ours—it is not limited to sympathy or acknowledgment. It is a knowing that enters in, bears with, and works mysteriously toward restoration. The wounds inflicted upon the vulnerable—by individuals, by systems, by those meant to shield instead of shatter—demand more than recognition. They demand redress. They demand justice. And sometimes, God's healing does not come as we imagine it: sometimes it does not erase the pain nor does it simply return us to innocence, yet there is most times if not always a deeper mending that holds the truth of what was broken.

It is one thing to suffer at the hands of the world—to face hardship, to encounter loss, to bear the burden of mortality. But it is another to suffer at the hands of those who were meant to protect. There is no pain more isolating, no wound more insidious, than betrayal by those who were supposed to be safe and keep us safe. Yet even in that desolation, God does not stand apart as a distant observer. God draws near to the places of devastation, making space for a new kind of wholeness—one that carries the memory of harm but is no longer defined by it. Betrayal does not merely wound. It rewrites the map of who we believe we are. The abused child, looking up into the eyes of the parent who was meant to protect and care for them. The parishioner, trusting the shepherd, only to be led to the slaughter. The student, the patient, the believer, placing their faith in a system and institutions that crumble under the strain of their own corruption.

These are but some of the wounds that do not simply ache, they reshape us. They steal our sense of safety, they distort our understanding of love, they make trust feel like a forgotten language. And too often, they are met not with justice but with silence; with denial, and with cover-ups and whispered apologies that come too late, if they come at all.

This is not new. The Bible is filled with warnings against those who prey upon the vulnerable, who exploit power for their own gain. The prophets cried out against corrupt leaders, against priests who defiled the sacred, against those who devoured the weak while claiming to serve God.

"Woe to the shepherds who destroy and scatter the sheep of my pasture!" (Jeremiah 23:1).

Austin once spoke of justice. Once sat in rooms where the sins of others were weighed and measured. Once passed judgment without hesitation. And now? Now, he is the one scattered. Now, he is the one waiting for a verdict. He writes,

"I won't ask for sympathy. I won't even ask for understanding."

But what does he ask for, then? To be remembered? To be forgiven? To be seen for more than his worst moment? But if we remember only his suffering, do we forget the suffering of the ones he silenced? How many others have been cast out with less mercy? How many others have been left to carry the consequences of actions that were not their own? The children, left with the burden of knowing. The woman, reduced to a whisper, a scandal, a cautionary tale. The family, now forced to reconcile the man they loved with the man they now see him to be. Because in truth this is the man he has always been. And by his actions, these too are the ones who have been scattered. These are the ones who bear the true burden of exile. And yet, still, the destruction continues. Still, the scattered sheep wander, broken and unseen. But they are not unseen by God. For every cry that has been silenced, there is God who hears. For every child who was abandoned, there is the Comforter who never leaves. For every wound inflicted by those in power, there is the hand of God, the healer that binds up the brokenhearted. But the work of justice is not only God's. It is also ours.

The Bible speaks not only of comfort but of responsibility. It commands us to defend the weak, to stand for the oppressed, to refuse complicity in systems that enable harm. It calls for restitution, for restoration, for a world where those who have been wronged do not simply survive but are made whole. And that is where we have failed. Not only in allowing harm to happen. But in the way we have sometimes excused it. In the way we have oftentimes allowed grace to become a shield for the guilty instead of a refuge for the wounded.

In recent years, organizations and advocates have risen in response to this call. Child protection services, victim advocacy groups, legal reforms—all striving to hold the guilty accountable and shield the innocent. Churches and faith communities, once silent in the face of abuse, are increasingly beginning to speak. Survivors are lifting their voices, breaking generations of silence. Laws are changing. Systems are shifting. But it is not enough. What has been broken cannot be undone, but it can be acknowledged. It can be met with action. It can be answered with something more than hollow apologies.

Justice requires more than words—it requires change. It requires accountability. It requires that those who have suffered do not simply hear that they are believed, but know that they are restored. That their pain is met, not with dismissal, but with tangible reparation. That their suffering is not buried beneath bureaucracy and excuses but faced, unflinchingly, with the full force of truth. And yet, even with justice, even with change, there remains the question of healing. Because trauma does not vanish with conviction. Suffering does not end with acknowledgment. The wounds inflicted in childhood do not disappear with age. The scars left by betrayal do not fade overnight. Austin will live with what he has done. That is his burden. But what of those he has harmed? What of those who must now find a way to live with what was done to them? This is where the Bible does not fail us. Because it does not promise immediate healing, but it does promise presence. It does promise that we do not walk through suffering alone. It tells us that exile is not forever. That the wilderness leads to the Promised Land. That the cross is followed by resurrection. It tells us of a God who gathers the broken, who binds the wounds of the afflicted, who walks with us through the valley of the shadow of death and does not leave us there. And sometimes, that is enough. Sometimes, that is everything.

Healing is not a straight path. It is not a singular moment. It is a journey—one that is often slow, often fraught, often filled with setbacks. But it is possible. With truth. With justice. With faith. For those of us who have known trauma, who have felt like strangers in our own lives, we find a home—not in a world that often fails us, but in a God who does not turn away from pain. A God who took suffering and transformed it. A God who says,

"I see you. I know what you have endured. And you are not alone."

And if there is anything we need to believe, it is that. Because in a world that so often abandons its wounded, there is One who never will.

A Bruising of Heaven

2:00 PM

The train has entered a stretch of countryside that feels almost abandoned—bare trees, broken fences, rusting outbuildings that might once have been chapels. I glance up and catch a glimpse of a steeple, half-collapsed, its cross still clinging to the roofline like a question. I think of all the places that once offered sanctuary. And how often we have used them to cover harm.

I return to Austin's letter. The edges are soft now from being folded and unfolded. My eyes land again on a line I cannot seem to forget:

"I believed in the order of things."

It's the kind of sentence that lingers not because it's profound—but because it sounds like a confession trying not to be one. He believed, once. And now? I exhale slowly, and the window fogs just slightly. The train rumbles on beneath me. We are a world gone wrong. The Word spoke us into being, and in the beginning, we were good. Creation was good—declared so by the very Word of God. The mountains, the rivers, the creatures moving across the earth, the first breath of humankind—all of it, good. And yet, we are no longer good. Not in the way we were made to be. We have twisted ourselves away from the original design, away from the harmony that once was. We have taken the gifts of creation and used them to destroy. We have turned on each other, betrayed one another, waged war, enslaved, oppressed, and built a world where suffering is more familiar than peace.

If we, made in God's image, can be traumatized—then what of God? What does it mean for the Creator to witness creation unravel? What does it mean for God to have breathed life into us, only to watch us use that breath to curse, to kill, to deny God's presence? We have made cruelty ordinary. We have made injustice efficient. We see glimpses of divine sorrow in scripture. We see it in Genesis 6, when God looks upon the earth and grieves at what humanity has become:

"The Lord saw that the wickedness of humankind was great in the earth . . . and it grieved God to the very heart" (Genesis 6:5–6).

We see it in the prophets, when Israel turns away again and again, and God cries out like a wounded lover:

"How can I give you up, O Ephraim? How can I hand you over, O Israel? My heart recoils within me; My compassion grows warm and tender" (Hosea 11:8).

We see it in Christ, standing on the hill overlooking Jerusalem, weeping:

"O Jerusalem, Jerusalem . . . how often I would have gathered your children together as a hen gathers her brood under her wings, and you were not willing!" (Matthew 23:37, Luke 13:34).

And we see it in the silence of the cross, when the world did its worst to the very Word of God. The bruising of heaven is not just grief. It is the sound of love being rejected.

Yes, we have traumatized God.

Because we have turned away. Because we have tried to fashion a god in our own image, a god that fits within the limits of our understanding, one that suits our desires. Because we have set up kingdoms for ourselves and called them divine. Because we have made war and claimed it was holy. Because we have shaped our religion the same way we tried to shape God . . . in our own image. And still, God pursues us.

The church exists to bring us back to God, to encourage, to enliven, to inspire, to show in action the love, mercy, and compassion of God. We were not made for religion. Religion was made for us. We had fallen so far that we needed something . . . some structure, some order, some practice . . . to help us remember who we were meant to be. A way to lead us back into communion with God. But too often, religion has failed. Not because it was broken in itself, but because we have broken it. We have used it to build walls instead of bridges, to claim power instead of offering grace. And so it was not effective enough. It could not heal the rift between us and God. It could not restore the communion that was lost.

Not until Christ.

Not until the Word Godself entered the world. Not until God became flesh and dwelt among us. Not until the great mystery unfolded—the infinite clothed in mortality, the uncontainable confined to a womb, the Creator walking among the created. Not until the fullness of God's love was revealed in the form of a man who healed the sick, lifted the lowly, and shattered the chains of sin. Not until we saw with our own eyes what God had always intended.

Not until we rejected Him.

The trauma continued as God chose to send God's Word, which accomplishes what it was sent to do. And to compound the trauma, we crucified our very Maker. This is who we are. We are the ones who nailed love to a tree. We are the ones who shouted for blood, who traded the Messiah for a murderer. We are the ones who mocked Him, God in the flesh as He gasped for breath. We are the ones who turned our backs as the sky grew dim. We are the ones who spat in the face of the One who called us beloved. And yet, the nature of God is not to abandon what was declared good. The same Word that called creation good is the same Word that stepped into the brokenness to free it. The same Word that breathed life into humanity is the same Word that took on flesh and hung on a cross for hours to bring us back to life. Because God's Word does not fail. It does not fade. It does not lose its power, even when we reject it. And so, after the work of the Word, after the cross, after the resurrection, after the work to release us from sin—after all of this, do we dare to believe that God's original word about us still stands? Even now? Even after everything?

And yet, when God looks at us now, what does God see? Through Christ, through the Word, through the work that has been done by the Christ, God sees us as we were always meant to be.

Still good.

Certainly not because of anything we have done, but because of what God has done. Because the Word cannot be undone. Because when God declared creation good, it was not a temporary truth. It was an eternal one.

We are a world gone wrong, yes. But we are also a world that has been released. Freed. Restored. The questions now are, will we step into the goodness that has been restored? Will we live as those who have been made whole? Will we return to the harmony that once was? Or will we continue to grieve the heart of God and continue to crucify the Christ who came to set us free? We still do these things when we choose greed over generosity, whenever we harden our hearts instead of extending grace, each time we close our eyes to suffering, justify injustice, exalt power over love and deny the presence of God in those who bear God's image. We crucify Christ again and again. And yet, still, God loves us. Still, God calls us back. Still, the invitation stands.

To come home.

To be healed.

To be made new.

To finally, fully, step into the communion that was always meant to be.

The bruising of heaven has not undone the blessing of heaven. It has only made the invitation more fierce, more urgent, more filled with grace. And maybe then, when we finally say yes, when we finally surrender to the love that has been pursuing us since the beginning, when we finally stop wounding the heart of God—maybe then, we will know peace. Maybe then, we will know joy and be able to look upon one another and see, truly see, what God has always seen. Maybe then, we will finally be able to speak the truth and call ourselves "good."

The train shifts gears as we begin another descent. I close Austin's letter gently, but my hands do not stop trembling. I whisper—not a prayer for comfort, but for courage. There is still time before we arrive. Still time to decide what kind of shepherd I will be.

Shared Breath, Shared Pain, Shared Grace

I slip Austin's letter into my pocket. The train hums beneath me, a steady rhythm threading my thoughts together, though the words he wrote still hover in the air around me like smoke.

"I believed in the order of things."

And now? Now we are all sitting in the ruins of an order we once trusted.

A message pings on my phone. It is from Paige. Five words: "You carry my love, prayers."

I read it twice, and I let the words steady me. And yes, I carry Paige's love and prayers, and I carry the love of wider family too and still I carry other things—I carry the question of faith.

I carried this question beyond my own reflections, beyond the walls of my church, beyond the borders of my own experiences. I took it across oceans, across histories, across cultures—to family in St. Vincent and to friends and strangers in Ghana. Particularly to Ghanaian university professors in theology and philosophy. I carried it because I wanted to understand: Why is it that after facing so much trauma and oppression, my family members and large numbers of people in Ghana still have faith in God? The answers I received pointed to two main truths. First, as they regained control of their land and country, the Ghanaians say that it gave them a sense of pride and achievement. Oppression had taken much from

57

them, but it had not taken their identity. Their faith, then, was not one of passive endurance—it was faith reinforced by action, by resilience, by the knowledge that survival is a form of defiance. But most of all, they spoke of community. They said the people possess a deep understanding of their connection to one another, to family, to history. They do not walk through trauma alone. Their suffering is not an isolated burden but one carried together, lightened by shared hands. When one person falls, another is there to lift them. When one grieves, the whole community grieves. And when faith falters, it is not left to die in silence—others stand in the gap, others pray, others remind them that even in suffering, they are not abandoned. Faith that is isolated is faith that is vulnerable. But faith that is a profound part of the fabric of a people, passed from hand to hand, generation to generation, carried in song, in memory, and in the quiet presence of a loved one sitting beside you in your lowest hour—that faith does not break easily. It bends, perhaps. It questions. It grieves. But it does not shatter. Because it was never meant to be carried alone.

And this is where my own family comes into focus—not as an abstract symbol of tradition, but as the living, breathing testament to that communal strength. Our closeness is not just emotional; it is spiritual, ancestral, and deeply rooted in memory. It is in the way we gather around food, laughter, and sometimes even debate, knowing that disagreement is not division. It is in the way we honor the stories of those who came before us, not as distant memories, but as guidance for the future. Their prayers did not just survive history. They built a road through it.

When I sit with my family—whether around a table or in quiet conversation — I feel the presence of those who prayed us into being. I feel the gravity of sacrifices made and the unspoken love that binds us. Even when we do not see eye to eye, even when the paths we take diverge, there is an undercurrent of belief—not just in God, but in each other. A belief that whatever storms we face, we do not face them alone.

This love is not fragile. It endures through pain, through distance, through time. It echoes with the voices of ancestors who survived for our sake, who endured so we could hope. It informs our faith not just in a higher power, but in the power of unity. It is in these bonds, reaching back generations, that we find the courage to face what lies ahead. The past gives us our roots, but it is love—alive and shared—that gives us our wings.

This memory of who we are, held in common, keeps our faith alive, not as a . . . The train shifts and rocks slightly forward, breaking my sentence in half. A soft, almost unbearable announcement crackles over the intercom:

"Next stop . . . Junction . . . ten minutes."

I look out the window and I see the landscapes slipping past in a blur of motion and color. I shift my bag slightly, feeling its heft, though it is nothing compared to the burden of thought pressing against my chest.

I think of Ghana. I think of Osu Castle. I had not expected to visit that place. I had not known what it truly was until I stood within its walls. Osu Castle—a large set of buildings, once closed to the public, the seat of government. I had been granted access through a Ghanaian colleague. What I did not know at the time was that Osu Castle was once an enslavement castle.

I was given a personal tour. Together, the guide, my Ghanaian colleague and me bore witness to a list of harms, such as: the chapel opposite the dungeons; the hole where captured women were entombed as punishment if they did not want to do as the castle warden demanded; the low, shadowy, cramped cells that were designed to force captured men to remain bent over so that they would grow weaker each day and not have the strength to fight for their God-given freedom, and the huge ponds built on top of the dungeons to muffle the screams, so that villagers outside would not hear what was happening beneath their feet. The tunnels that carried the captured into the castle were hidden from the eyes of the world, but never from the eyes of God.

Everything about the architecture symbolized for me instruments of dehumanization. Tools of terror, crafted to silence, subjugate, and erase. And yet—they could not erase the image of God in those whose cries were swallowed by water and stone. As I walked through the chambers, I could feel each place saturated in sorrow. On the floors were remnants of skin, blood, tears and 'excrement' still there after so many years. A site where human evil reached a crescendo so deafening that only God's compassion could hold the echoes.

I kept thinking: the chapel was opposite the dungeons. What kind of person worships God while inflicting suffering? Worship above. Suffering below. Praise sung above screams.

And still—God was there.

In agony.

Crushed.

Because that is the God we see in Jesus—a God who descends, who enters the dungeon, who bears the weight of injustice and does not look away. This is not a history we move past without bearing witness to those who survived it, and those who did not.

It is a grief we carry.

But we do not carry it alone.

We carry it with the Christ who was crucified by empire. We carry it with the Spirit who groans with us. We carry it with the God who still asks:

"The voice of your brother's blood is crying to me from the ground" (Genesis 4:10).

And we remember—redemption does not come by forgetting. It comes by naming what was done, lamenting what was lost, and refusing to let death have the final word.

And the Door of No Return.

I stood there.

I felt the air, thick with memory.

There are places where history does not fade; places where time lingers, where suffering seeps into the stone, where the silence is not empty but full—

full of names, full of cries, full of prayers.

And I prayed.

My prayers now added to my ancestors prayers in that place. A place where even the walls remember. The gravity of that place settled over me like a weight. I thought about the hands that had pressed against those walls, the feet that shuffled forward in chains, toward a future stolen by greed, toward ships that smelled of death, toward a door that would erase their homeland, their language, their names—but never their dignity. I could sense the urgency of the last prayers whispered in there, prayers spoken into uncertainty, into terror. Prayers for courage, for release, perhaps, but certainly for God to still be near.

And God was.

Not on the side of the captors. Not in the false faith that justified chains with scripture and hymns. No—God was in the chains, in the crushed bodies and the crying mothers, in the last breath of a child whose name only God remembered. Because that is the God we know in Christ, not a God who stays distant, but one who enters the sorrow, who bears wounds, who is nailed down and yet never defeated. And even there—faith remained. Not the faith of those who put up the walls, but the faith of those they tried to destroy. A faith that refused to be extinguished, that flowed into whispered songs, into the grip of one shackled hand holding another, and into stories told in the shadows and hymns sung in defiance. A faith passed down through oceans, through generations, into grandmothers' prayers over sleeping children, into the quiet, stubborn praise sung on Sunday mornings by a people who still fought to remember who they were—and whose they were. A faith not born of safety, but forged in suffering. A faith that endured because their love refused to surrender. And because—though they were told otherwise—God had never let them go.

The train continues to hum a steady rhythm beneath my thoughts. A quiet, even heartbeat. I touch the outside of my coat pocket, where Austin's letter now rests.

There is a word in the Akan language: Sankofa. It means "go back and fetch it." It is a call to remember, to retrieve what has been lost, to look back—not to be trapped in sorrow, but to gather what is needed to move forward.

Faith, in many ways, is family to Sankofa.

It looks back. It acknowledges. It does not forget. And it demands that we learn in order to go forward.

I shift in my seat, the weight of a different thought settling in. There is a meeting ahead. A meeting of ministers. A gathering of voices who will speak of faith, of leadership, and of what it means to shepherd others in the name of God. But there is a sickness that must be spoken of. There are those who have worn the title of minister and used it to wound instead of heal. There are those who have betrayed the trust placed in them, who have taken advantage of the vulnerable, who have covered sin in robes of false righteousness.

Faith is not only about endurance. It is also about accountability. I think of Osu Castle again. I think of the chapel that stood opposite the dungeons. Prayers rising above suffering. But what is the worth of prayer if it rises from lips of hypocrisy? What does it mean to pray when injustice remains unchallenged? What does it mean when faith is used as a shield for those who harm? I do not yet know what will be said in the meeting. But I know this: Faith must not be silent. It must not be used as a cloak for injustice. It must have the courage to look into the shadowy places, to call out what must be called out, to demand truth where lies have taken root.

I think of the people of Ghana. Their faith did not survive by ignoring the truth. It survived because they carried it together, held one another accountable and refused to let suffering be forgotten. And so, I know what must be done. Faith is not merely belief. It is the courage to stand in the presence of injustice and say, no more. It is the willingness to bear witness—to what has been done, to what must change, to what must never be allowed to happen again. It is the responsibility to ensure that the next generation inherits not just faith, but a faith that is worthy of trust. I open my notebook and write one sentence at the top of the page:

"When I speak, I will not soften the truth."

The train moves forward, carrying me toward what lies ahead.

The Breath That Remains

2:40 PM

An uninvited cough stirs in my throat, unwelcome, unprovoked. I press my fingers against my lips, willing it to pass, willing my lungs to behave. The air inside the train is warm, close, thick with the quiet murmurs of passengers and the rustling of newspapers. A tight pressure clamps around my ribs, every breath shallow and ragged. I need to be off this train, out where the cool air can fill my lungs. Instead I am trapped.

This body of mine, this vessel that carried me through sickness and into survival, is still at war with itself. The scars on my lung are invisible to others, but I feel them with every breath. I close my eyes.

Breathe in.

Breathe out.

It is enough.

Some days, it is all I can manage. And some days, "enough" feels like defiance. But then I remember—breath is no small thing. It is the first thing we are given when we enter this world, the last thing we surrender when we leave it. It is the Spirit of God moving over the waters in the beginning, the wind that parted the sea, the breath breathed into dry bones in Ezekiel's vision. It is what Jesus gave up on the cross when he said,

"It is finished" (John 19:30).

Breath is life itself. And yet, I know what it is to be without it. I know what it is to wake in the night, lungs locked, panic seizing my chest. I know what it is to gasp for air that does not come, to fight for something that should be effortless.

I think of her. Betty. She never knew how much she was appreciated. She thought herself a troublemaker, a difficult member of the church, a woman whose opinions made her a burden. But she was not. She was honest. She was fair. She was filled with humor and conviction and integrity. The call came at 11:00 pm. She was in hospital, and she was dying. Her family member's voice carried the burden of love that knew it was running out of time. I dressed quickly. There was no question—I had to go. The night was deep and still as I stepped outside, but inside me, the urgency hummed. I drove through streets that felt too empty, too slow, pressing forward toward the place where she lay between this world and the next. When I arrived, her family was gathered. The room was thick with waiting, with grief that had not yet found its voice. And then—her eyes opened. She saw me. And even now, in this moment of departure, she was still in character, her mischievous comment was:

"What are you doing here? You should be in bed. You need your rest."

I smiled. She gave a weak chuckle, the kind that barely touches the lips but carries years of understanding. She knew.

She knew she was leaving. And I knew it too. Breath is not ours. It belongs to God. It is on loan, carried in our lungs for as long as we are given. That night, I watched as her breath thinned, slowed, became a whisper of what it once was. Until finally, it stopped. It did not belong to her. It never did. And yet, the life she lived, the fire in her, the love she gave—it was real. It remains.

Every breath leaves a trace. Every love leaves a mark. At her funeral, her granddaughter approached me with something in her hand. A pin. A small character with a mischievous smile.

"She asked me to give this to you," Betty's granddaughter said. "She wanted you to wear it at the funeral. She wanted you to remember her—on your shoulder, always giving trouble or always stating her opinion."

I took it. And for a moment, I could almost hear her laugh. What does this say about breath? That it lingers. That though it is not ours to keep, it leaves traces behind. That even when it ceases in the body, it continues in the love we have given, the mischief we have stirred, the words we have spoken in truth.

The train jolts slightly, pulling me back. I shift in my seat, watching the world move past in blurred streaks of color. The rhythm of the train matches the rhythm of my breath, steady now, measured.

I think of another home. Another family. Another time of grief. Another moment. I entered the home of Mary and Gavin, where breath felt thin, not because of illness but because of the heaviness of life itself. Gavin, Mary's husband, was dying. I arrived at the house, expecting quiet, expecting the hush that grief often brings. But inside—chaos. Papers, books, bags, cups, clothes—all stacked, piled, spread across every surface. There was nowhere to sit.

"One moment," Mary said, clearing a chair, shifting things just enough to make space. Then, she called upstairs.

"Bring it down!" she shouted.

Her daughter did not walk down. She did not come gently, carrying whatever it was. Instead, she threw it. From the top of the stairs, an object tumbled down, knocking against steps, landing hard at the bottom. A lever arch file, a record of monies collected for the community aid work of the church. No pause. No reverence. No care. Some houses are filled with grief loud enough to shatter walls . . . and quiet enough to be missed. I saw it then—how breath can be stifled even in the living. How some homes are filled with suffocation, not because the air is thin but because the spirit is burdened. I did not ask questions. I did not need to. I stayed. I prayed. I took the file. I breathed for them in the space where their own breath felt too burdened to rise.

The train shudders again, an announcement crackling through the speakers. We are approaching my stop. And yet, I am still on the journey. Breath is not ours. It belongs to God. But while we have it, what do we do with it? Do we waste it on passing blame, on grudges, on holding our breath in anger or fear? Or do we use it to speak truth, to lift others, to fill rooms with laughter and kindness and conviction? Betty in the hospital bed—she used hers well. Mary in the cluttered house—she struggled beneath the burden of hers. And I?

I am still learning.

Still breathing.

Still on the train, moving forward.

The doors will open soon. I will step off. And I will breathe for as long as God allows. And when the time comes to surrender this borrowed breath back to The One who gave it, may it be said that I used it well.

The train slows. I rise. The journey continues.

Marked By Time

3:00 PM

The train glides into the station, the metal wheels sighing against the tracks like a weary traveler coming to rest. The carriage shudders, and for a moment my body sways with it, unsteady, remembering—always remembering that stillness is never truly still. I exhale, slow and careful, as the doors slide open. The scent of the city rushes in, damp stone and diesel, the salt-wind drifting up from the water's edge. I step forward.

The station is a cathedral of movement, a vast hall of steel and glass where voices rise and fall like a chanted prayer. Announcements echo from unseen speakers, their sharp syllables distorted by the cavernous space. Trains come and go, pulling in with a groan, departing with a sigh—endless arrivals, endless departures. Posters line the walls, their bright colors clashing, advertising distant places, cheap travel, the promise of escape. Others are less welcoming—warnings, regulations, reminders of what cannot be brought beyond these doors. Above them, the great iron beams stretch across the ceiling, rib-like, holding the burden of a hundred years of comings and goings. The station holds its history like a breath held too long. Beneath the polished floors, there are layers of another time, another world. The workers who laid these tracks, backs bent, hands calloused, their sweat soaking into the stone. The evacuees who once stood on these platforms, small suitcases clutched in trembling hands, gas-mask boxes swinging at their sides. The soldiers who left and never returned. And now, there is me.

My bag pulls at my shoulder, the strap digging in as I step forward. I move carefully, navigating the shifting currents of bodies, weaving through travelers who walk without hesitation, without thought, their lungs full, their steps sure. My own breath is measured, deliberate, a rhythm I must control lest my body reminds me of its limits. The steps come into view, and my chest tightens in anticipation. They descend to the lower road, leading into the heart of the city, into the pulse of the mid-afternoon crowd. I pause at the top, adjusting the load on my shoulder, steeling myself. The stone beneath my feet is worn, smoothed by a thousand thousand footsteps. The history of every footfall is beneath me, and now, mine will join them.

One step.

A pause. A breath drawn and released.

Another.

The road below is alive with sound—the call of street vendors, the laughter of children, the impatient horns of cars caught in afternoon traffic. The scent of food drifts upward—spiced meat, fried batter, something sweet and unfamiliar. A city's hunger in the air. I reach the bottom of the steps, and the street unfolds before me, a river of people moving in all directions. There is a rhythm to the city, a beat I must match. I walk, slow but steady, letting the current pull me forward.

The buildings tower on either side, their glass windows catching the last of the sun. But among them, older faces remain—stone facades carved with names long forgotten, doorways that once welcomed another kind of traveler. There is beauty here, in the old and the new pressed together, in the way history refuses to be erased. Ahead, the great churches rise, their spires reaching toward the heavens they claim to represent. Their stained-glass windows are dark now, the light behind them extinguished, but I know the stories they hold. Their walls have seen too much.

There was a time when these churches were filled with those who sought refuge, who fell to their knees in whispered prayer, their hands clasped in desperate supplication. But there was another time, too. A time when these same walls housed silence. When they turned away from the suffering within their own midst, when their doors were closed to those who needed them most.

I think of the meeting ahead—of the voices that will fill the room, speaking of justice, of change, of all the things that should have been done but were not. I think of my colleagues—some righteous in their anger, others complicit in their silence. I think of the suffering we will discuss—not abstract, not distant, but real, present, breathing among us. Vulnerable adults, wounded children now grown, carrying the burden of harm done in places that claimed to be safe. The failure to see, the failure to act, the refusal to acknowledge, and the ones who still suffer, the ones who cannot walk into a church without the past rising like smoke in their lungs. The past does not sleep inside these walls. It waits. It demands. I know what it is to carry wounds that will not close.

I thought of John, a young man I often visited, at the care home where he resided. He was in his late twenties, yet living among the elderly—a placement that felt like a sentence he hadn't earned. John was depressed, restless. He had been a motorcycle enthusiast once, before the accident that cost him part of his skull. The doctors called his wound healed, but it still oozed. There were gaps in his head, in his memory, in his speech, in his life. He spoke often of his family, bitter that they had placed him there. He longed to be around people his own age, to feel some spark of belonging again. He asked me to speak with them, his family members, to reason with them, to encourage them to move him from this place. He wanted to go home. He wanted to feel the warmth of eating with family around the table and laying in his own familiar bed at night. His life was fragile. So were his emotions.

I went away on holiday for a few weeks. When I returned, John was gone. He had laid his burden down. Some wounds never close. Some lives end before there is time to heal, leaving spaces that cannot be filled. But I have learned that sometimes, even in the ruins, something new can take root.

The road ahead curves toward such a place—a church, or what remains of one. Its walls stand, hollowed by fire and time, stone scarred by the war that tore through this city. No roof remains, only sky above, open and endless. But where once there was ruin, now there is art. Where once the silence was a weight, now voices rise—not in prayer, but in poetry, in music, in the raw expression of those who refuse to be forgotten. Artists gather here, their work displayed against ancient stone, their words echoing where hymns once rang. Actors perform beneath the open sky, their voices carrying stories of love, of loss, of struggle. It is a holy place, still. But not because of what was, or what was lost. But because of what has been reclaimed. I stop for a moment, my breath shallow, my lungs protesting the journey. I press a hand to my chest, feeling the steady beat beneath my palm. My body remembers too much. It carries the scars of battles fought and won, but victory does not come without cost.

The meeting awaits. But for now, I stand in the ruins, breathing-in the echoes of what was and what will be. The city is alive, shifting, changing, refusing to be held in the past. And so am I. I am alive, too. Scarred, breathless, marked by time. But alive. For now, that is enough.

Breathless, But Not Broken

3:15 PM

The incline stretches before me, silent and unyielding. It is not steep, not the kind that forces knees to nearly kiss the ground in surrender, but it is long—deceptively long. A slow, relentless rise that does not announce itself as a challenge until you are in the middle of it, lungs tightening, breath shortening, the body realizing too late that there is no quick way to the top. Can I make it? Would the breath hold? Would the body that had survived so much finally betray me now? There was no guarantee. Only the climb.

I pause at the base, shifting the load of the duffel bag on my shoulder. The strap bites into my skin, the dull ache blooming sharper as I roll my shoulder forward. A reminder of what I carry, of what I have always carried. I draw in a breath. The air is heavier here, thick with something I cannot name. It is not the city's smog nor the closeness of too many bodies exhaling in unison. No, this burden is different. It is the density of expectation, the pressure of what awaits at the top. I grip the strap tighter. Victory is not the absence of wounds. It is carrying them and still moving forward. One step.

The pavement beneath me is uneven, worn smooth in some places, treacherous in others where time and weather have cracked its surface. My foot lands carefully, and I shift my balance forward. The air is sharp against my skin, cool in a way that makes movement feel sluggish, like wading through unseen waters. The cold does not refresh; it presses down, stealing heat from my breath, making the climb harder.

Another step.

The incline is no longer just a stretch of pavement—it becomes something more, something older, something I have faced before in a thousand different ways. The incline was not just a stretch of pavement; it was every hardship stitched into my bones. Every silent battle no one had seen. Every scar hidden under polite smiles. I think of the nights in hospital, when breathing felt like a battle waged in the space between sleep and waking. The way my lungs would seize, grip tight around air that refused to move. The quiet panic that came with the knowledge that my own body was a traitor. I think of the woman who once sat in my office, her hands twisting in her lap, her voice barely above a whisper.

"Every day feels impossible."

She had not come for solutions. She had not come for empty words, for scriptures pulled from a book and placed before her like bandages over a wound too deep to close. I did not tell her to be strong. I did not tell her that God never gives us more than we can bear. I did not tell her that it would get better. I simply said:

"Then just take the next step. That's all. Just one more step."

Now, I tell myself the same.

Another step.

The incline does not end. It stretches, expands, becomes eternal.

My muscles protest, the ache shifting from discomfort to something more insistent. My breath comes in shorter draws now, controlled but deliberate. I count each inhale, each exhale, measuring them against my steps, trying to maintain a rhythm, but not succeeding. The duffel bag grows heavier. At the bottom of the incline, it was manageable. Now, with each step, it feels like it gathers mass, filled with something more than its physical contents. I wonder if I should have packed lighter. And I wonder, not for the first time, what it would be like to set it down. What if I reached the top without it? What if I let it go? But there are things you carry because they are part of you now; things you do not simply set aside because the journey is hard.

Grief.

Memory.

The burden of survival.

I shift the bag again, ignoring the sting in my shoulder, the way my spine curves slightly beneath the strain. I have carried heavier things.

Another step.

The city behind me grows distant, the sounds of traffic and conversation fading into something muffled, distorted. The world is narrowing, focusing. There is only this path. Only this moment. Only the climb.

I think of others who have climbed inclines of their own. The woman from my congregation, who stood at the edge of a decision that would change everything. Who faced the impossible and chose to walk forward anyway. She told me once that faith is not loud, not a grand declaration, nor a battle cry. It is quiet. A whisper in the shadows. A step taken when standing still would be easier. I wonder if she knew then that I needed to hear it as much as she did. Because there is a moment—halfway up the incline—when I think about stopping. It is not dramatic. There is no great collapse, no sudden gasp of exhaustion. Just the thought: I could stop now. I could rest. And beneath it, quieter but there nonetheless: Would it matter? Because how many battles have I fought only to find another battle waiting? How many times have I reached the top only to realize there is still another hill ahead? The weight on my back wasn't just the duffel bag anymore. It was regret. It was memory. It was the fear that this climb—this life—was already too much.

I slow my steps, my breath labored now, the strain of everything pressing down.

The bag.

The journey.

The expectation.

The fact that at the top of this incline, I must face something that will demand of me more than just my breath. And there, at the edge of doubt, something else stirs.

Beyond defiance.

Beyond determination.

Memory.

I remember the first breath I took after the doctor told me the cancer was gone. I remember the pressure of my mother's hand in mine the last time we prayed together. I remember the woman who said,

"Every day feels impossible," and the way she nodded—just slightly—when I told her that all she had to do was take the next step. I remember that she did. And so do I.

Another step.

The faces of those I'd seen fall flickered in my mind. Some had slipped quietly. Some had raged against the incline until there was nothing left. Which would I be? And again, I think of Austin. He had not just stumbled. He had collapsed under the full weight of his own choices, and dragged others down with him.

"I don't know why I'm writing. Maybe because there's no one left to listen. Maybe because silence has never suited me, and yet now it is all I have."

His letter still sits in my coat pocket, yet the weight of it seems to press against my spine. I remember the conference room were together we once convened a meeting, I remember the discussions we once had, the way his voice carried certainty where mine carried questions. Austin had walked up his own inclines. But in the end, had he stopped climbing? Maybe he had been pushed down. Maybe his burden had become too great. Maybe his steps had slowed, and no one noticed. Or worse—no one cared to notice. And so, at the very end of himself, when the incline stretched before him and he had no more steps to take, he wrote to me saying :

"I knew the order of things. I believed in it once."

But belief is a fragile thing. It does not hold up well to the weight of consequence

"I won't ask for sympathy. I won't even ask for understanding. I only ask this—when they speak my name, when they tally my failures, let there be one among you who remembers: I was not always this."

I close my eyes, feeling the heft of his words, of the truth he carried for too long. And then, I take another step. Because his story is not mine to carry. But the lesson is.

Another step.

But what of the children? What of the ones who opened that vestry door and saw not a sanctuary, but a place of ruin? There are moments that split time in two—before and after. For them, that moment was one. The laughter they once brought to Junior Church, the trust with which they had entered that church, the belief they had in the sacredness of that space—it all fractured in an instant. What they saw was not just two bodies entwined. They saw betrayal, hypocrisy, the collapse of something they had been told was unshakable.

Austin, the minister.

And her—a leader, a mother, a wife to a man who already hated the church and now had reason to. Their betrayal was not in secrecy alone, but in exposure—in the harm done to those who should never have borne witness. What burden do these children now carry? It is heavier than the duffel on my back. It is the kind of burden that shapes a soul before it even fully forms. Their incline is longer, steeper. It is not measured in steps, but in sleepless nights, in questions with no safe answers, in families who now speak of faith in past tense. Their parents, once proud to walk them through church doors, now hesitate, uncertain if trust can ever be restored. And the children—do they look to the cross and wonder if God was watching, and if so, why God did not intervene?

Trauma is a heavy thing. It lingers, seeps into the crevices of memory, coils itself around the heart. For some, the climb will be too great. Others will stumble, falter. But a few—perhaps just a few—will find the strength to begin, to rise, to take one more step. Not because they forget. But because they refuse to be defined by what was done to them. Because survival is not submission. Because healing is rebellion. Every step they take, back toward life is an act of defiance against the ones who wounded them. Because even on a broken path, ascent is possible.

The top is closer now, though my body does not yet believe it. The incline is flattening, the path steadying beneath me. The load has not lessened, but I no longer think about putting it down. Because this climb is not just for me. It is for those who have climbed before me. It is for those still standing at the bottom, wondering if they have the strength to begin. It is for the ones who were told they would not make it. It is for the ones who are still trying to believe that victory does not mean walking unscathed, but walking at all.

The final steps are slow, deliberate. I reach the top. The incline levels out beneath my feet. I pause. Breathe in. Breathe out. And then—the door opens.

Austin's story does not end with him, but with them—with the children, those families, now standing at the foot of their own incline. He fell. And in that fall, he sent ripples through a community that will likely never be the same. But where he stopped climbing, they begin. Their journey is the true incline—one scarred by betrayal, shadowed by loss—yet still possible. And maybe that is the only victory left to claim. That despite it all, they climb.

One step.

Then another.

And another.

Until the door opens for them—not to a memory of pain—but to something new. Something earned. Something sacred again.

My colleagues are there. At the open door. Two of them. They see what I did not want them to see. I was gasping for air. I could feel the contortions in my face stretched, searching for breath—for a heartbeat, and I wonder if they see more than my breathlessness. Do they see how close I came to stopping altogether? Their eyes scan my face, my posture. They see the strain I carry, they witness the labor of my breathing. I try to act normal, but my body won't let me. I feel disheveled, my senses heightened, but yet not fully aware of everything that surrounds me. One of them asks,

"Are you alright? Can I get you some water?"

Another doesn't wait for an answer — she just disappears down the hallway, returns with water. I try to speak to let them know that I'll be okay. But it's easier to nod. I take the water, my fingers curling around the cup. The condensation against my palm feels grounding, a small mercy. My throat is tight, breath ragged. But the sip steadies me. Then I hear it, softly:

"You'll be okay."

I nod in agreement. Now catching my breath, Now feeling much better. The meeting waits behind another door.

They wait.

Life waits.

And I—I just stand there, in the aftermath.

Not triumphant. Not unscathed. But upright. Because I climbed. Because the broken can still climb. There's nothing doctors can do. I've got to live with this. For now I'm still breathing. For now, I'm still living.

I will telephone Paige and let her know I have arrived.

The Voice That Speaks

3:20 PM

We do not grasp the ways of God, even as we wrestle with the reality of a God who is present in our pain. And yet, we begin to see that divine presence is not distant or abstract—it is tangible, unyielding, and constant. Still, we feel uncertain when we cry out and are met with silence, when the ruins of trust seem beyond rebuilding—yet deep within, we sense this truth: it is into that very silence that God speaks first.

God is the voice that speaks when all other voices have fallen silent. God is the presence that does not waver, does not abandon, does not shift with the rising and falling tides of human frailty. If the world is a place of breaking, then God is the one who remains in the aftermath. If suffering is the condition of humanity, then God is the one who steps into it—out of love, without endorsing it, and without being indifferent to it, enduring it without justifying it, choosing to be present within it. To be near. To be with. A bruised world, a broken people—and still, God refuses to walk away. This is the God revealed in the Bible—not a God who remains distant, waiting for humanity to rise to perfection before drawing near, but a God who walks through every valley, who is never absent from struggle, who does not abandon even the ones who falter. It does not say, if you are without flaw, you will be well. It does not say, if you are strong enough, holy enough, perfect enough, I will be with you. God's presence is not conditional.
It simply is.

God's love does not waver with human success or failure.
God remains.

And this is the truth that upends every notion of justice, every human measure of worthiness, every attempt to make God's love something earned rather than something that simply is.

There are those who suffer and believe they have been forgotten. They carry wounds that will not close, burdens that cannot be spoken, histories that stretch far beyond their own lifetimes. The world tells them their suffering is their own to bear, that struggle is simply the nature of things. And sometimes, even faith communities—even those who claim to know the nature of God—will speak of suffering as though it is a test to be endured rather than a burden that should have never been placed upon them. But God does not stand at a distance, measuring suffering from afar. God inexplicably steps into it—and with us, endures it, suffers it. If God is with us, then we are not forsaken. If God walks in our midst, then our suffering is seen. God is not in the systems that oppress, not in the hands that wound, not in the cruelty of those who turn away. God is in the endurance. God is in the breath that still remains. God is in the ones who do not let go. And if God has seen, then justice and mercy are not illusions. Justice is not an idea written on pages of law books or spoken in courts where the powerful decide the fate of the weak. Justice is the very nature of God. Justice is the gravity of divine presence among those who have been cast aside. And if God is there, then suffering does not have the final word. The ones who have been crushed will rise. The ones who have been silenced will sing. The ones who have been cast aside will stand in the presence of The One who never turned away.

But what of the ones who have done wrong? The ones whose hands have left bruises, whose silence has become complicity? What of those who have failed—not only in small ways, not only in quiet moments of human weakness, but in ways that have harmed others, that have left wounds where there should have been healing? What of Austin and the woman and the harm done to the children and all the families affected—not seeking restoration, not asking to be absolved, but simply because he now knows the burden of his own failure? There are those who would say that such a person should not be named among the people of faith. That to fall in this way is to be cast out, to be placed beyond the reach of grace. And yet—not one. Not even the ones who have fallen furthest; not even the ones who have done harm are exempt from finding forgiveness in God.

The scandal of God's grace is that it stoops lower than we believe it ever could or should. Does this mean that justice is undone? No! Does this mean that suffering is erased? No! But it means that God does not abandon. Even those who have done wrong, even those who must face the consequences of their own actions, are still seen. Still called. Still given breath. God does not restore the unjust to power, does not erase the consequences of sin, does not pretend that harm was never done. But God does not let go. Even those who have fallen are not forgotten. Even those who have failed are not left to perish. Because grace is not something that can be exhausted. Because mercy is not something that runs out. Because God is still present, even the worst of human failure is not beyond freeing. This is not a freeing that restores power or wipes away accountability. But one that calls even the most fallen back into truth. It is the kind of freedom that says: you cannot undo what has been done, but you can face it — with honesty, with humility, and with God still near. You can bear the responsibility of it. You must repent of it. And you are not alone in that burden. There is no promise that suffering will end today. There is no promise that the load will be lifted in a single moment, that all burdens will suddenly disappear. What is promised is presence. What is promised is endurance. What is promised is that the ones who hold on will not be forsaken. And this is why faith endures. Not because it has always been easy. Not because justice has already been fulfilled. Not because the wounds have all been healed. But because God is still here.

Still walking among those who suffer.

Still calling those who have failed.

Still breathing life into those who thought they could not continue.

Still daring us to believe that the broken will not stay broken.

And so the road stretches ahead, not yet complete, not yet free of struggle.

But God walks it.

And because of that, there will be victory. Not the kind of victory that erases scars. Not the kind of victory that undoes the past. But the kind of victory that means the past does not have the final word. The kind of victory that means suffering does not own the future. The kind of victory that means those who endure will rise. Because God is with them. Because God has always been with them. Because God will remain. And because of that, the journey is not over. Not for any of us.

The Light Within

It is with this hope—this fierce, unwavering presence—that we step forward, carrying not only the burden of suffering, but also the light that refuses to be extinguished. I have climbed the incline. I have borne the weight. I have walked into rooms where justice and silence fought for dominance, where people chose comfort over truth, where suffering was acknowledged with words but ignored with actions. I have sat with those who no longer trust. I have listened to stories whispered through gritted teeth, stories of betrayals wrapped in Scripture, wounds inflicted by the very hands meant to heal. I have seen faith twisted into a shelter for the powerful, and a weapon against the vulnerable. And still—I believe.

I believe because there is a light that remains. It is not a light that erases suffering. It is not a light that denies the reality of what has been done. It is a stubborn, relentless light—a light that refuses to be put out.

Remember Moses, his face radiant as he descended the mountain, carrying the unbearable glory of what he had seen. And the people—afraid—begged him to cover the light. To veil his face. To make it more palatable. And I wonder—how often have we done the same? How often have we dimmed the truth to make it less disruptive? How often have we spoken of love without justice, grace without accountability? How often have we wrapped the light in veils because it exposed too much—our failures, our betrayals, our silence when it mattered most? How often have we stood, like them, trembling before the brightness of truth, and chosen to step back into the shadows?

But the light remains.

Even when we cover it.

Even when we deny it.

Even when we turn away.

The disciples saw Jesus transfigured on the mountain. They saw, with their own eyes, the glory that had always been there, hidden beneath the flesh of His humanity. And what did they want to do?

Contain it.

Capture it. Stay where it was safe, where it was breathtaking, where it demanded nothing from them but wonder. But faith was never meant to stay on the mountain. It is meant to descend into the world.

This faith is meant to go into the alleyways where suffering still lingers. Into the courtrooms where justice has been delayed. Into the whispered conversations where truth must be spoken even when it costs everything. For many that is a big ask. Into the lives of those who have been harmed, not with platitudes, but with presence. With courage. With hands that refuse to let go. Even when it would be easier to turn back. Even when silence would protect us. Even when pretending would save our reputation. Because that is not faith. Faith does not let us forget.

Faith does not allow us to bless injustice with our silence. Faith does not leave us as we are. Faith drags us into the shadowed places—not to be overcome by them, but to bear light within them. We go as those shaped by humility, as those acquainted with struggle, as those who keep standing, even when faltering seemed easier, as those who have seen the light—and are learning to walk in it. We go as those who know, just as Moses knew, that God is the God not only of light, but of shadow, for while the people remained at a distance, trembling, Moses approached the thick darkness where God was. And because God is God, because God is in control in light as in darkness, we can never again pretend that the world is beyond hope.

I don't know how much more must break before healing begins. I don't know how long the wilderness will stretch before us. I don't know how many more betrayals or nights of grief we will have to bear. But I do know this: A light remains — steady, unwavering, not of our making. It remains because God is faithful. Because God does not turn away. Because God holds sorrow without letting it have the final word.

The door to the meeting stood open before me. I cross the threshold, breathing steady now, though the ache in my chest still pulsed with every step. The room was already half-full, colleagues gathered around the table, voices low, papers spread before them like battle plans. I found a seat against the wall, letting the duffel bag slip from my shoulder with a soft thud. Around me, the meeting unfolded. Time stretched and blurred, swallowed by reports, procedural debates, the details of cases read out in solemn tones. No names called. Some details . . . I barely knew. Others hit closer to the bone. And then, the context of the story I knew it was Austin's. The air shifted, almost imperceptibly, as the details of his case were spoken aloud. The facts laid bare. The harm named. He was not the only one to be discussed that day, but his failure was the deepest cut for me. He was a colleague I thought I knew. We were never close, but we worked well together. We had stood together in better times. Now, I sat listening as the consequences of his choices were weighed. The discussion was heavy, careful, almost clinical. But beneath the formal language, the room carried an ache that no minutes or motions could disguise. And then, although I was not prepared to speak on this matter and the names were kept anonymous, I felt it necessary to speak about the injustice to shed light and not be silent.

I rose, not with a grand speech prepared, not with righteous fury bottled and ready to pour out, but with the quiet fire that had been forged in the climb, in the broken places, in the rooms where silence had already done enough damage. I spoke for the children who could not un-see what they had seen. I spoke for the families who now questioned what sacredness meant. I spoke for those whose breath still caught in their throats when they crossed the threshold of a church. And although Austin's name sat heavy on my heart, I spoke not so much for him, but for all who bore the wounds his betrayal had deepened. I spoke because the light demands it. And though not everyone listened, though some shifted uncomfortably, and others looked away, the truth was spoken aloud, and it could not be taken back.

Not now.

Not ever.

The light moved forward that day, not in triumph, but in persistence. And that is how the world is remade: Not all at once.

But breath by breath.

Step by step.

Truth by truth.

And so . . . we walk forward. Not yet fully healed. Not yet fully whole. But carrying the light, however we can, for as long as breath remains in our lungs. The story is not over, because even in the valley of shadow, the light still burns, and because the light can never . . . will never . . . be put out. And yet, even as the room emptied and the night drew close, I knew, the light was not the end of the story. It was only the beginning of what must come next.

The decisions still waited. The reckonings still demanded courage. The wounded still deserved more than silence. Tomorrow would rise. And with it, the call to keep walking. It was only the first breath of a longer journey. Tomorrow, the work would continue. Tomorrow, we would sit again around the heavy tables, Tomorrow, the hard decisions would call us by name. Tomorrow, the wounded would still wait for someone to stand with them. Weighing failures against hope, grief against justice, truth against the fragile scaffolding of what remained. Healing would not be handed out easily—it would be chosen, fought for, built brick by aching brick. But tonight, there was breath. Tonight, there was the flicker of a light not extinguished.

As I stepped outside into the gathering dusk, I felt it—the crackle of something more. Not resolution. Not certainty. But the unmistakable pulse of hope, stubborn and alive. We had not solved everything. We had not healed everything. But we were still here.

Tomorrow would come, and when it did, we would be ready—because the light still burns. And yes there will be reckonings. There will be reckonings for Austin, for the others, for all who had wounded and all who had borne the wounds. There would be tears yet unshed, questions yet unanswered, paths yet to be cleared. But there would also be light. There would be the breath of those still standing; the strength of those still speaking; the fire of those who refused to let wrongdoing have the final word. Tomorrow would ask everything of us. We will continue to answer. We continue to climb. We continue to carry the light forward into a world still breaking, continuing to be remade. Because the story was not over. Because God is not finished. And with God's help, neither are we.

Breath by breath.

Step by step.

Light by relentless light, we continue.

This is the measure of breath:

Not merely survival.

Not merely endurance.

But carrying hope into all that still aches to be made whole.

I measured breath in pain.

I measure it now in light.